Odd Interlude

Dean Koontz is the author of more than a dozen *New York Times* No.1 bestsellers. His books have sold over 450 million copies worldwide, a figure that increases by more than 17 million copies per year, and his work is published in 38 languages.

He was born and raised in Pennsylvania and lives with his wife Gerda and their dog Anna in southern California.

Also by Dean Koontz

Odd
Interlude

Dean Koontz

HARPER

This novel is entirely a work of fiction.
The names, characters and incidents portrayed in it are
the work of the author's imagination. Any resemblance to
actual persons, living or dead, events or localities is
entirely coincidental.

Harper
An imprint of HarperCollins*Publishers*
77–85 Fulham Palace Road,
Hammersmith, London W6 8JB

www.harpercollins.co.uk

HarperCollins*Publishers*
Macken House, 39/40 Mayor Street Upper,
Dublin1, D01 C9W8, Ireland

Published in Great Britain by HarperCollins*Publishers* 2012

20

Copyright © Dean Koontz 2012

Dean Koontz asserts the moral right to
be identified as the author of this work

A catalogue record for this book
is available from the British Library

ISBN: 978-0-00-750864-8

Set in Old Style 7 by Palimpsest Book Production Limited,
Falkirk, Stirlingshire

Printed and bound in the UK using 100% renewable
electricity at CPI Group (UK) Ltd

MIX
Paper from
responsible sources
FSC® C013604

PART ONE

South of Moonlight Bay

Oh! They're too beautiful to live,
much too beautiful.

—Charles Dickens, *Nicholas Nickleby*

One

THEY SAY THAT EVERY ROAD LEADS HOME IF you care to go there. I long for home, for the town of Pico Mundo and the desert in which it blooms, but the roads that I take seem to lead me to one hell after another.

In the front passenger seat of the Mercedes, through the side window, I watch the stars, which appear to be fixed but in fact are ever moving and perpetually receding. They seem eternal, but they are only suns that will burn out one day.

When she was just a child, Stormy Llewellyn lost her mother, Cassiopeia. I lost Stormy when she and I were twenty. One of the northern constellations is called Cassiopeia. No group of distant suns is named for Stormy.

I can see Cassiopeia's namesake high in the night, but

I can see Stormy only in my memory, where she remains as vivid as any living person I might meet.

The stars and everything else in the universe began with the big bang, which was when time also began. Some place existed before the universe, exists outside of it now, and will exist when the universe collapses back upon itself. In that mysterious place, outside of time, Stormy waits for me. Only through time can time be conquered, and the way forward is the only way back to my girl.

Yet again, because of recent events, I have been called a hero, and again I don't feel like one.

Annamaria insists that mere hours earlier, I saved entire cities, sparing many hundreds of thousands from nuclear terrorism. Even if that is most likely true, I feel as though, in the process, I have forfeited a piece of my soul.

To foil the conspiracy, I killed four men and one young woman. They would have killed me if given a chance, but the honest claim of self-defense doesn't make the killing lie less heavily upon my heart.

I wasn't born to kill. Like all of us, I was born for joy. This broken world, however, breaks most of us, grinding relentlessly on its metaled tracks.

Leaving Magic Beach, fearing pursuit, I had driven the Mercedes that my friend Hutch Hutchison lent me. After several miles, when the memories of recent violence overwhelmed me, I stopped along the side of the road and changed places with Annamaria.

Now, behind the wheel, by way of consolation, she says, "Life is hard, young man, but it was not always so."

I have known her less than twenty-four hours. And the longer I know her, the more she mystifies me. She is perhaps eighteen, almost four years younger than me, but she seems much older. The things she says are often cryptic, though I feel that the meaning would be clear to me if I were wiser than I am.

Plain but not unattractive, petite, with flawless pale skin and great dark eyes, she seems to be about seven months pregnant. Any girl her age, in her condition, alone in the world as she is, ought to be anxious, but she is calm and confident, as if she believes that she lives a charmed life— which often seems to be the case.

We are not linked romantically. After Stormy, there can be none of that for me. Although we do not speak of it, between us there is a kind of love, platonic but deep, strangely deep considering that we have known each other such a short while. I have no sister, although perhaps this is how I would feel if I were Annamaria's brother.

Magic Beach to Santa Barbara, our destination, is a four-hour drive, a straight shot down the coast. We have been on the road less than two hours when, two miles past the picturesque town of Moonlight Bay and Fort

Wyvern—an army base that has been closed since the end of the Cold War—she says, "Do you feel it pulling at you, odd one?"

My name is Odd Thomas, which I explained in previous volumes of this memoir, which I will no doubt explain again in future volumes, but which I will not explain here, in this detour from the main arc of my journey. Until Annamaria, only Stormy called me "odd one."

I am a short-order cook, though I haven't worked in a diner since I left Pico Mundo eighteen months earlier. I miss the griddle, the deep fryer. A job like that is centering. Griddle work is Zen.

"Do you feel it pulling?" she repeats. "Like the gravity of the moon pulling tides through the sea."

Curled on the backseat, the golden retriever, Raphael, growls as if in answer to Annamaria's question. Our other dog, the white German shepherd named Boo, of course makes no sound.

Slumped in my seat, head resting against the cool glass of the window in the passenger door, half hypnotized by the patterns in the stars, I feel nothing unusual until Annamaria asks her question. But then I sense unmistakably that something in the night summons me, not to Santa Barbara but elsewhere.

I have a sixth sense with several facets, the first of which is that I can see the spirits of the lingering dead, who are reluctant to move on to the Other Side. They often want me to bring justice to their murderers or to help them find the courage to cross from this world to the next. Once in a while, I have a prophetic dream. And since leaving Pico Mundo after Stormy's violent death, I seem to be magnetized and drawn toward places of trouble, to which some Power wishes me to travel.

My life has mysterious purpose that I don't understand, and day by day, conflict by conflict, I learn by going where I have to go.

Now, to the west, the sea is black and forbidding except for a distorted reflection of the icy moon, which on those waters melts into a long silvery smear.

In the headlights, the broken white line on the blacktop flashes toward the south.

"Do you feel it pulling?" she asks again.

The inland hills are dark, but ahead on the right, pools of warm light welcome travelers at a cluster of enterprises that are not associated with a town.

"There," I say. "Those lights."

As soon as I speak, I know we will find death in this place. But there is no turning back. I am compelled to act in these cases. Besides, this woman seems to have become my backup conscience, gently reminding me what is the right thing to do when I falter.

A hundred yards past a sign that promises FOOD FUEL

LODGING, an exit from the highway looms. She takes it fast, but with confidence and skill.

As we reach the foot of the ramp and halt at a stop sign, I say, "You feel it, too?"

"I'm not gifted as you are, odd one. I don't feel such things. But I know."

"What do you know?"

"What I need to know."

"Which is?"

"Which is what is."

"And what is this what-is that you know?"

She smiles. "I know what matters, how it all works, and why."

The smile suggests she enjoys tweaking me by being enigmatic—although there is no meanness in her teasing.

I don't believe there is any deception in her, either. I am convinced she always speaks the truth. And she does not, as it might seem, talk in code. She speaks the truth profoundly but perhaps as poets speak it: obliquely, employing paradox, symbols, metaphors.

I met her on a public pier in Magic Beach. I know nothing of substance about her past. I don't even know her last name; she claims that she doesn't have one. When I first saw Annamaria, I sensed that she harbored extraordinary secrets and that she needed a friend. She has accepted my friendship and has given hers to me. But she holds tightly to her secrets.

The stop sign is at an intersection with a two-lane county road that parallels the state highway. She turns left and drives toward a service station that is open even in these lonely hours before dawn, offering a discount brand of gasoline and a mechanic on call.

Instead of a double score of gasoline pumps that a truck stop might offer, this station provides just four pumps on two islands. At the moment, none is in use.

Dating from the 1930s, the flat-roofed white-stucco building features Art Deco details, including a cast-plaster frieze revealed by lights in the overhanging cornice. The frieze depicts stylized cars and borzoi hounds racing perpetually, painted in yellows, grays, and royal blue.

The place is quaint, a little architectural gem from an age when even humble structures were often artfully designed and embellished. It is impeccably maintained, and the warm light in the panes of the French windows no doubt looks welcoming to an average traveler, although nothing here charms *me*.

Intuition sometimes whispers to me but is seldom loud. Now it is equivalent to a shout, warning me that although this place might be pleasing to the eye, under the attractive surface lies something terrible.

In the backseat, Raphael growls low again.

I say, "I don't like this place."

Annamaria is unperturbed. "If you liked it, young man, there'd be no reason for us to be here."

A tow truck stands beside the station. One of the two bay doors is raised, and even at this hour, a mechanic works on a Jaguar.

A nattily dressed man with a mane of silver hair—perhaps the owner of the Jaguar, recently rescued from the side of the highway—stands watching the mechanic and sipping coffee from a paper cup. Neither of them looks up as we cruise past.

Three eighteen-wheelers—a Mack, a Cascadia, and a Peterbilt—are parked on the farther side of the station. These well-polished rigs appear to belong to owner-operators, because they have custom paint jobs, numerous chrome add-ons, double-hump fenders, and the like.

Beyond the trucks, a long low building appears to be a diner, in a style matching the service station. The eatery announces itself with rooftop red-and-blue neon: HARMONY CORNER / OPEN 24 HOURS. Two pickups and two SUVs are in front of the diner, and when Annamaria parks there, the Mercedes' headlights brighten a sign informing us that for cottage rentals we should inquire within.

The third and final element of this enterprise, ten cottages, lies past the restaurant. The units are arranged in an arc, sheltered under mature New Zealand Christmas trees and graceful acacias softly but magically lighted. It appears to be a motor court from the early days of automobile travel, a place where Humphrey Bogart might hide out with Lauren Bacall and eventually end up in a gunfight with Edward G. Robinson.

"They'll have two cottages available," Annamaria predicts as she switches off the engine. When I start to open my door, she says, "No. Wait here. We're not far from Magic Beach. There may be an all-points bulletin out for you."

After thwarting delivery of the four thermonuclear devices to terrorists, mere hours earlier, I'd called the FBI office in Santa Cruz to report that they could find four bomb triggers among the used clothing in a Salvation Army collection bin in Magic Beach. They know I'm not one of the conspirators, but they are eager to talk with me anyway. As far as the FBI is concerned, this is prom night, and they don't want me leaving the dance with anyone but them.

"They don't know my name," I assure Annamaria. "And they don't have my picture."

"They might have a good description. Before you show yourself around here, Oddie, let's see how big a story it is on the news."

I extract my wallet from a hip pocket. "I've got some cash."

"So do I." She waves away the wallet. "Enough for this."

As I slump in the dark car, she goes into the diner.

She is wearing athletic shoes, gray slacks, and a baggy sweater that doesn't conceal her pregnancy. The sleeves are too long, hanging past the first knuckles of her fingers. She looks like a waif.

People warm to her on sight, and the trust that she inspires in everyone is uncanny. They aren't likely to turn her away just because she lacks a credit card and ID.

In Magic Beach, she had been living rent-free in an apartment above a garage. She says that although she never asks for anything, people give her what she needs. I have seen that this is true.

She claims there are people who want to kill her, but she seems to have no fear of them, whoever they might be. I have yet to see proof that she fears *anything*.

Earlier, she asked if I would die for her. Without hesitation, I said that I would—and meant it.

I don't understand either my reaction to her or the source of her power. She is something other than she appears to be. She tells me that I already know what she is and that I only need to accept the knowledge that I already possess.

Weird. Or maybe not.

Long ago, I learned that, even with my sixth sense, I am not a singularity and that the world is a place of layered wonders beyond counting. Most people unconsciously blind themselves to the true nature of existence, because they fear *knowing* that this world is a place of mystery and meaning. It's immeasurably easier to live in a world that's all surfaces, that means nothing and demands nothing of you.

Because I so love this wondrous world, I am by nature optimistic and of good humor. My friend and mentor Ozzie Boone says buoyancy is one of my better qualities. However, as though to warn that excess buoyancy might lead to carelessness, he sometimes reminds me that shit, too, floats.

But on my worst days, which are rare and of which this is one, I can get down so low that the bottom seems to be where I belong. I don't even want to look for a way up. I suppose surrender to sadness is a sin, though my current sadness is not a black depression but is instead a sorrow like a long moody twilight.

When Annamaria returns and gets behind the wheel, she hands me one of two keys. "It's a nice place. Sparkling clean. And the food smells good. It's called Harmony Corner because it's all owned and operated by the Harmony family, quite a big clan judging by what Holly Harmony told me. She's the lone waitress this shift."

Annamaria starts the Mercedes and drives to the motor court, repeatedly glancing at me, which I pretend not to notice.

After she parks between two cottages and switches off

the engine and the headlights, she says, "Melancholy can be seductive when it's twined with self-pity."

"I don't pity myself," I assure her.

"Then what would you call it? Perhaps self-sympathy?"

I decide not to answer.

"Self-compassion?" she suggests. "Self-commiseration? Self-condolence?"

"I didn't think it was in your nature to needle a guy."

"Oh, young man, I'm not needling you."

"Then what would you call it?"

"Compassionate mockery."

The landscape lamps in the overhanging trees, filtering through leaves that quiver in a gentle breeze, flutter feathery golden light across the windshield and across Annamaria's face and surely across my face as well, as if projected upon us is a film involving winged multitudes.

I remind her, "I killed five people tonight."

"Would it be better if you had failed to resist evil and had killed no one?"

I say nothing.

She persists: "Those would-be mass murderers . . . do you suppose they would have surrendered peacefully at your stern request?"

"Of course not."

"Would they have been willing to debate the righteousness of the crimes they intended to commit?"

"The mockery I get, but I can't see how it's compassionate."

She is unrelenting. "Perhaps they would have been willing to go with you on that TV-courtroom show and let Judge Judy decide whether they did or did not have the moral authority to nuke four cities."

"No. They'd be too scared of Judge Judy. *I'm* scared of Judge Judy."

"You did the only thing you could have done, young man."

"Yeah. All right. But why do I have to go from Magic Beach to Harmony Corner in the same night? So much death. No matter how bad those people were, no matter how bad someone might be here . . . I'm not a killing machine."

She reaches out to me, and I take her hand. Although I can't explain why, the very contact lifts my spirits.

"Maybe there won't be any killing here," she says.

"But it's all accelerating."

"What is?"

"My life, these threats, the craziness—coming at me like an avalanche."

The feathers of soft light flutter not just across her face but also in her eyes as she squeezes my hand. "What do you most want, Oddie? What hope drives you? The hope of a little rest, some leisure time? The hope of an uneventful, quiet life as a fry cook, a shoe salesman?"

"You know it's none of that."

"Tell me. I'd like to hear you say it."

I close my eyes and see in memory the card that came out of a fortune-telling machine in a carnival arcade six years earlier, when with Stormy at my side I had bought a precious promise for a quarter.

"Ma'am, you know what the card said—'You are destined to be together forever.' "

"And then she died. But you kept the card. You continued to believe in the truth of the card. Do you still believe in it?"

Without hesitation, I reply: "Yes. I've got to believe. It's what I have."

"Well then, Oddie, if the hope that drives you is the truth of that card, might not the acceleration that frightens you be what you actually want? Might you be quickening toward the fulfillment of that prediction? Could it be that the avalanche coming at you is nothing more than Stormy?"

Opening my eyes, I meet her stare once more. The fluttering wings reflected on her face and in her dark eyes might also be the flicker of golden flames. I am reminded that fire not only consumes; it also purifies. And another word for purification is *redemption*.

Annamaria cocks her head and smiles. "Shall we find a castle with a suitable room where you can do your version of Hamlet's most famous soliloquy to your heart's content? Or shall we just get on with this?"

I am not out of smiles, after all. "We'd best be getting on with it, ma'am."

Our only luggage is a hamper of food for us and the golden retriever, which was packed by our friend Blossom Rosedale in Magic Beach. After Raphael finds a patch of grass in which to pee, I follow the dog and Annamaria to Cottage 6, which she has taken for herself, and I leave the hamper with her.

On the stoop, delivery made, as I turn away, she says, "Whatever happens here, trust your heart. It's as true as any compass."

The white German shepherd, Boo, has been with me for several months. Now he accompanies me to Cottage 7. Because he is a ghost dog, he has no need to pee, and he walks through the door before I can unlock it.

The accommodations are clean and cozy. Sitting area, bedroom alcove, bath. The unit seems to have been remodeled and upgraded within the past few years.

There's even an under-the-counter fridge that serves as an honor bar. I take a can of beer and pop the tab.

I am exhausted but not sleepy. Now, two hours before dawn, I've been awake twenty-two hours; yet my mind spins like a centrifuge.

After switching on the TV, I sit with the remote in an armchair, while Boo explores every cranny of the cottage, his curiosity as keen in death as in life. Satellite service provides a huge smorgasbord of programming. But nearly everything seems stale or wilted.

As far as I can tell from the cable-news channels, the thwarted nuclear terrorists in Magic Beach have not made the news. I suspect they never will. The government will decide that the public prefers to remain ignorant of such disturbing near disasters, and the political class prefers to *keep* them ignorant rather than arouse in them suspicions of corruption and incompetence in high places.

On NatGeo, in a documentary about big cats, the narrator informs us that panthers are a variety of leopard, black with black spots. A panther with golden eyes stares directly at the camera, bares its fangs, and in a low, rough voice says, "Sleep."

I realize that I am less than half awake, in that twilight consciousness where dreams and the real world sometimes intersect. Before I drop off and spill the beer, I put the nearly empty can on the table beside the armchair.

On the screen, a panther seizes an antelope with its claws, pulls the prey off its feet, and tears out its throat. The graphic violence does not shock me awake but instead weighs on me, wearies me. Lifting its head, the triumphant cat stares at me, blood and saliva drizzling from its mouth, and says, "Sleep . . . sleep."

I can feel the words as well as hear them, sound waves issuing from the TV speakers, pulsing through me, a kind of sonic massage that relaxes my tense muscles, soothes the taut fibers of my nerves.

Several hyenas test the panther as it drags the antelope into a tree to feed on it in higher branches where neither these wolfish rivals nor lions—which also do not climb— are able to follow.

A hyena, wild-eyed and loathsome, bares its ragged teeth at the camera and whispers, "Sleep." The rest of the pack repeats the word, "Sleep," and the sonic waves quiver through me with a most pleasing narcotic effect, as does the voice of the panther in the tree, while the head of the antelope lolls on its ruined neck, its fixed eyes glazed with the most perfect sleep of all.

I close my eyes, and the panther of the waking dream follows me into slumber. I hear the soft but heavy padding of its paws, feel its sinuous form slinking through my mind. For a moment, I am disquieted, but the intruder purrs, and its purring calms me. Now the big cat is climbing into another tree, and although I am not dead, the creature carries me with it, for I am powerless to resist. I am not afraid, because it tells me that I should have no fear, and as before, not just the meaning of the words but also the sound waves of which they are formed seem to oil the waters of my mind.

This is the tree of night, black branches reaching high into the starless sky, and nothing can be seen but the panther's lantern eyes, which grow in size and brightness until they are owlish. In that low, rough voice, it says, *Why can't I read you?* Perhaps it is neither owl nor panther, because now I feel what seem to be fingers, as if I am a book of countless pages that are being turned, pages that prove to be blank, the fingers sliding across the paper as if seeking the raised dots of a biography in braille.

The mood changes, the would-be reader's frustration is palpable, and in the darkness, the eyes are suddenly green with elliptical pupils. If this is a dream, it's also something more than a dream.

Although a dream shapes itself and can't be consciously scripted by the dreamer, when I wish for light, I have the power to call it forth. Darkness begins to recede from the tangled black limbs of the tree, and the shape of the would-be reader begins to coalesce out of the gloom.

I am *thrust* awake, as if the mysterious figure in the nightmare has thrown me out of it. I scramble to my feet, aware of movement to my right, at the periphery of vision, but when I pivot toward it, I find myself alone.

Behind me, something thrums, as if a pair of practiced hands are strumming arpeggios from a harp with only bass strings. When I turn, no origin of the sound is obvious—and now it arises not from where it had been but from the alcove in which stands the bed.

Seeking the source, I am led into the alcove and then to the bathroom door, which is ajar. Darkness lies beyond.

In my exhaustion and emotional confusion, I have forgotten my pistol. It's tucked under the front passenger seat of the Mercedes.

The gun once belonged to the wife of a minister in Magic Beach. Her husband, the reverend, had shot her to death before she could shoot him. In their particular denomination of Christianity, the faithful are evidently too impatient to wait for prayer to solve their problems.

I push open the bathroom door and switch on the lights. The thrumming swells louder, but now comes from behind me.

Turning, I discover that Boo has returned, but he is not the primary point of interest. My attention is drawn to what has also transfixed the dog: a quick transparent *something*, visible only by the distortion that it imparts to things as it crosses the alcove, enters the sitting area, seems to spring into the TV screen without shattering it, and is gone.

That presence is so fast and shapeless, I half suspect that I have imagined it, except that the wildlife documentary on the TV ripples with concentric rings, as if the vertical screen is a horizontal body of water into which a stone has been dropped.

Blinking repeatedly, I wonder if what I'm seeing is real or if I have a problem with my vision. The phenomenon diminishes gradually until the images on the screen become clear and stable once more.

This was no ghost. When I see one of the lingering dead, it is the very image of the once-living person, and it doesn't move quicker than the eye can follow.

The dead don't talk, and neither do they make other sounds. No rattling of chains. No ominous footsteps. They have no weight to make the stair treads creak. And they certainly don't strum arpeggios from a bass-string harp.

I look at Boo.

Boo looks at me. His tail doesn't wag.

Two

I AM NOW WIDE AWAKE.

The dream of tree and panther lasted less than five minutes. I am still suffering serious sleep deprivation, but I am as alert as might be a man in a foxhole when he knows the enemy will charge at any moment.

Leaving the lights on rather than return to a dark cottage, I step outside, lock the door, and retrieve the pistol from under the passenger seat of the Mercedes.

I am wearing a sweatshirt over a T-shirt, and I tuck the pistol between them, under my belt, in the small of my back. It isn't an ideal way to carry a weapon, but I don't have a holster. And in the past, when I have resorted to this method, I have never accidentally shot off a chunk of my butt.

Although I don't like guns and do not usually carry one, and although killing even the worst of men in self-defense or in defense of the innocent leaves me sickened, I am not so fanatically antigun that I would rather be murdered— or watch a murder be committed—than use one.

Boo materializes at my side.

He is the only spirit of an animal that I have ever seen. An innocent, he surely has no fear of what he might face on the Other Side. Although he is immaterial and cannot bite a bad guy, I believe that he lingers here because there will come a moment when he will be Lassie to my Timmy and will save me from falling into an abandoned well or the equivalent.

Sadly, most kids these days don't know Lassie. The media dog that they know best is Marley, who is less likely to save children from a well or from a burning barn than he is to barf on them and accidentally start the barn fire in the first place.

The oppressive mood infecting me since recent events in Magic Beach seems to have lifted. Curiously, nothing restores my common sense and puts me back on the firm ground of reason like a creepy encounter with something apparently supernatural.

In the lighted branches of the trees, the weak breath of the night makes the leaves quiver as if in anticipation of an approaching evil. On the ground around me, trembling patterns of light and shadow create the illusion that the land is unstable underfoot.

In the arc of cottages, no lamps brighten any windows except those in my unit and Annamaria's, although five other vehicles are parked here. If those guests of the Harmony Corner motor court are sleeping, perhaps a secret reader pages through their memories and seeks . . . Seeks what? Merely to know them?

The reader—whoever or whatever it might be wants something more than to know me. As surely as the antelope in the documentary is a few days' worth of meals to the panther, I am prey, perhaps not to be eaten but in some way to be used.

I look at Boo.

Boo looks at me. Then he looks at Annamaria's lighted windows.

At Cottage 6, as I rap lightly on the door, it swings open as though the latch must not have been engaged. I step inside and find her sitting in a chair at a small table.

She has taken an apple from the hamper, peeled and sectioned it. She is sharing the fruit with Raphael. Sitting at attention beside her chair, the golden retriever crunches one of the slices and licks his chops.

Raphael looks at Boo and twitches his tail, happy that there's no need to share his portion with a ghost dog. All dogs see lingering spirits; they aren't as self-deluded about the true nature of the world as most people are.

"Has anything unusual happened?" I ask Annamaria.

"Isn't something unusual always happening?"

"You've had no . . . no visitor of any kind?"

"Just you. Would you like some apple, Oddie?"

"No, ma'am. I think you're in danger here."

"Of the many people who want to kill me, none is in Harmony Corner."

"How can you be sure?"

She shrugs. "No one here knows who I am."

"*I* don't even know who you are."

"You see?" She gives another slice of apple to Raphael.

"I won't be next door for a while."

"All right."

"In case you scream for me."

She appears amused. "Whyever would I scream? I never have."

"Never in your whole life?"

"One screams when one is startled or frightened."

"You said people want to kill you."

"But I'm not afraid of them. You do what you need to do. I'll be fine."

"Maybe you should come with me."

"Where are you going?" she asks.

"Here and there."

"I'm already here, and I've *been* there."

I look at Raphael. Raphael looks at Boo. Boo looks at me.

"Ma'am, you asked if I would die for you, and I said yes."

"That was very sweet of you. But you're not going to have to die for me tonight. Don't be in such a hurry."

I once thought Pico Mundo had more than its share of eccentric folks. Having traveled some, I now know eccentricity is the universal trait of humanity.

"Ma'am, it might be dangerous to sleep."

"Then I won't sleep."

"Should I get you some black coffee from the diner?"

"Why?"

"To help you stay awake."

"I suppose you sleep when you need to. But you see, young man, I only sleep when I want to."

"How does that work?"

"Splendidly."

"Don't you want to know why it could be dangerous to sleep?"

"Because I might fall out of bed? Oddie, I trust your admonition isn't frivolous, and I will remain awake. Now go do whatever you have to do."

"I'm going to snoop around."

"Then snoop, snoop," she says, making a shooing motion.

I retreat from her cottage and close the door behind me. Already Boo is walking toward the diner. I follow him. He fades away like fog evaporating.

I don't know where he goes when he dematerializes. Maybe a ghost dog can travel to and from the Other Side as he pleases. I have never studied theology.

For the last day of January along the central coast, the night is mild. And quiet. The air smells faintly, pleasantly, of the sea. Nevertheless, my sense of impending peril is so great that I won't be surprised if the ground opens under my feet and swallows me.

Big moths caper around the sign on the roof of the diner. Their natural color must be white, because they become entirely blue or red depending on which neon is closer to them. Bats, dark and changeless, circle ceaselessly, feeding on the bright swarm.

I don't see signs and portents in everything. The voracious yet silent flying rodents chill me, however, and I decide not to stop first at the diner, as had been my intention.

Past the three eighteen-wheelers, at the service station, the Jaguar is gone. The mechanic is sweeping the floor of the garage.

At the open bay door, I say, "Good morning, sir," as cheerfully as if a gorgeous pink dawn has already painted the sky and choirs of songbirds are celebrating the gift of life.

When he looks up from his work with the push broom, it's a *Phantom of the Opera* moment. A grisly scar extends from his left ear, across his upper lip, through his lower lip, to the right side of his chin. Whatever the cause of the wound, it appears as if it might have been sewn up not by a doctor but instead by a fisherman using a hook and a length of leader wire.

With no apparent self-consciousness about his appearance, he says, "Hello there, son," and favors me with a grin that would make Dracula back off. "You're up even before Wally and Wanda have thought about goin' to bed."

"Wally and Wanda?"

"Oh, sorry. Our possums. Some say them two is just big ugly red-eyed rats. But a marsupial isn't no rat. And ugly is like they say about beauty—it's in the eye of the beholder. How you feel about possums?"

"Live and let live."

"I make sure Wally and Wanda get the throw-away food from the diner each and every night. It makes 'em fat. But their life is hard, what with mountain lions and bobcats and packs of coyotes with a taste for possum. Don't you think possums they have a hard life?"

"Well, sir, at least Wally has Wanda and she has Wally."

Abruptly his blue eyes glimmer with unshed tears and his scarred lips tremble, as if he is nearly undone by the thought of possum love.

He appears to be about forty, though his hair is iron gray. In spite of the horrific scar, he has an avuncular quality suggesting that he's as good with children as he is kind to animals.

"You've gone right to the very heart of it. Wally has Wanda, and Donny has Denise, which makes anythin' tolerable."

Stitched on the breast pocket of his uniform shirt is the name DONNY.

He blinks back his tears and says, "What can I do for you, son?"

"I've been up awhile, need to stay awake awhile longer. I figure anyplace truckers stop must sell caffeine tablets."

"I've got NoDoz in the gum-and-candy case. Or in the vendin' machine, there's high-octane stuff like Red Bull or Mountain Dew, or that new energy drink called Kick-Ass."

"They really named it Kick-Ass?"

"Aren't no standards anymore, anywhere, in anythin'. If they thought it would sell better, they'd call the stuff Good Shit. Excuse my language."

"No problem, sir. I'll take a package of NoDoz."

Leading me through the garage to the station office, Donny says, "Our seven-year-old, he learned about sex from some Saturday-mornin' cartoon show. Out of nowhere one day, Ricky he says he don't want to be either straight or gay, it's *all* disgustin'. We unplugged our satellite dish. No standards anymore. Now Ricky he watches all them old Disney and Warner Brothers toons on DVD. You never have to worry if maybe Bugs Bunny is goin' to get it on with Daffy Duck."

In addition to the NoDoz, I purchase two candy bars. "Does the vending machine accept dollars or do I need change?"

"It takes bills just fine," Donny says. "Young as you look, you can't have been drivin' a rig long."

"I'm not a trucker, sir. I'm an out-of-work fry cook."

Donny follows me outside, where I get a can of Mountain Dew from the vending machine. "My Denise, she's a fry cook over to the diner. You got yourself your own private language."

"Who does?"

"You fry cooks." The two sections of his scar become misaligned when he grins, as if his face is coming apart like a piece of dropped crockery. "Two cows, make 'em cry, give 'em blankets, and mate 'em with pigs."

"Diner lingo. That's a waitress calling out an order for two hamburgers with onions, cheese, and bacon."

"That stuff tickles me," he says, and indeed he looks tickled. "Where you been a fry cook—when you had work, I mean?"

"Well, sir, I've been bouncing around all over."

"It must be nice seein' new places. Haven't seen no new place in a long time. Sure would like to take Denise somewhere fresh. Just the two of us." His eyes fill with tears again. He must be the most sentimental auto mechanic on the West Coast. "Just the two of us," he repeats, and under the tenderness in his voice, which any mention of his wife seems to evoke, I hear a note of desperation.

"I guess with children it's hard to get away, just you two."

"There's never no gettin' away. No way, no how."

Maybe I'm imagining more in his eyes than is really there, but I suspect that these latest unshed tears are as bitter as they are salty.

When I wash down a pair of NoDoz with the soda, he says, "You jolt your system like this a lot?"

"Not a lot."

"You do too much of this, son, you'll give yourself a for-sure bleedin' ulcer. Too much caffeine eats away the stomach linin'."

I tilt my head back and drain the too-sweet soda in a few long swallows.

When I drop the empty can in a nearby trash barrel, Donny says, "What's your name, boy?"

The voice is the same, but the tone is different. His affability is gone. When I meet his eyes, they're still blue, but they have a steely quality that I have not seen before, a new directness.

Sometimes an unlikely story can seem too unlikely to be a lie, and therefore it allays suspicion. So I decide on: "Potter. Harry Potter."

His stare is as sharp as the stylus on a polygraph. "That sounds as real as if you'd said 'Bond. James Bond.' "

"Well, sir, it's the name I've got. I always liked it until the books and movies. About the thousandth time someone asked me if I was really a wizard, I started wishing my name was just about anything else, like Lex Luthor or something."

Donny's friendliness and folksy manner have for a moment made Harmony Corner seem almost as benign as Pooh Corner. But now the air smells less of the salty sea than of decaying seaweed, the pump-island glare seems as harsh as the lights of an interrogation room in a police station, and when I look up at the sky, I cannot find Cassiopeia or any constellation that I know, as if Earth has turned away from all that is familiar and comforting.

"So if you're not a wizard, Harry, what line of work do you claim to be in?"

Not only is his tone different, but also his diction. And he seems to have developed a problem with his short-term memory.

Perhaps he registers my surprise and correctly surmises

the cause of it, because he says, "Yeah, I know what you said, but I suspect that's not the half of it."

"Sorry, but fry cook is the whole of it, sir. I'm not a guy of many talents."

His eyes narrow with suspicion. "Eggs—wreck 'em and stretch 'em. Cardiac shingles."

I translate as before. "Serving three eggs instead of two is stretching them. Wrecking them means scrambling. Cardiac shingles are toast with extra butter."

With his eyes squinted to slits, Donny reminds me of Clint Eastwood, if Clint Eastwood were eight inches shorter, thirty pounds heavier, less good-looking, with male-pattern baldness, and badly scarred.

He makes a simple statement sound like a threat: "Harmony doesn't need another short-order cook."

"I'm not applying for a job, sir."

"What *are* you doing here, Harry Potter?"

"Seeking the meaning of my life."

"Maybe your life doesn't have any meaning."

"I'm pretty sure it does."

"Life is meaningless. Every life."

"Maybe that works for you. It doesn't work for me."

He clears his throat with a noise that makes me wonder if he indulges in unconventional personal grooming habits and has a nasty hairball stuck in his esophagus. When he spits, a disgusting wad of mucus splatters the pavement, two inches from my right shoe, which no doubt was his intended target.

"Life is meaningless except in your case. Is that it, Harry? You're better than the rest of us, huh?"

His face tightens with inexplicable anger. Gentle, sentimental Donny has morphed into Donny the Hun, descendant of Attila, who seems capable of sudden mindless violence.

"Not better, sir. Probably worse than a lot of people. Anyway, it isn't a matter of better or worse. I'm just different. Sort of like a porpoise, which looks like a fish and swims like a fish but isn't a fish because it's a mammal and because no one wants to eat it with a side of chips. Or maybe like a prairie dog, which everyone calls a dog but isn't really a dog at all. It looks like maybe a chubby squirrel, but it isn't a squirrel, either, because it lives in tunnels, not in trees, and it hibernates in the winter but it isn't a bear. A prairie dog wouldn't say it was better than real dogs or better than squirrels or bears, just different like a porpoise is different, but of course it's nothing like a porpoise, either. So I think I'll go back to my cottage and eat my candy bars and think about porpoises and prairie dogs until I can express this analogy more clearly."

Sometimes, if I pretend to be an airhead and a bit screwy, I can convince a bad guy that I'm no threat to

him and that I'm not worth the waste of time and energy
he would have to expend to do bad things to me. On
other occasions, my pretense infuriates them. Walking
away, I half expect to be clubbed to the ground with a
tire iron.

Three

THE DOOR TO COTTAGE 6 OPENS AS I APPROACH it, but no one appears on the threshold.

When I step inside, closing the door behind me, I find Annamaria on her knees, brushing the golden retriever's teeth.

She says, "Blossom once had a dog. She put an extra toothbrush in the hamper for Raphael, and a tube of liver-flavored toothpaste."

The golden sits with head lifted, remarkably patient, letting Annamaria lift his flews to expose his teeth, refraining from licking the paste off the brush before it can be put to work. He rolls his eyes at me, as if to say *This is annoying, but she means well.*

"Ma'am, I wish you'd keep your door locked."

"It's locked when it's closed."

"It keeps drifting open."

"Only for you."

"Why does that happen?"

"Why shouldn't it?"

"I ought to have asked—*how* does that happen?"

"Yes, that would have been the better question."

The liver-flavored toothpaste has precipitated significant doggy drool. Annamaria pauses in the brushing and uses a hand towel to rub dry the soaked fur on Raphael's jaws and chin.

"Before I went snooping, I should have warned you not to watch television. That's why I came back. To warn you."

"I'm aware of what's on TV, young man. I'd as soon set myself on fire as watch most of it."

"Don't even watch the good stuff. Don't switch it on. I think television is a pathway."

As she squeezes more toothpaste onto the brush, she says, "Pathway for what?"

"That's an excellent question. When I have an answer, I'll know why I've been drawn to Harmony Corner. So how does the door open just for me?"

"What door?"

"This door."

"That door is closed."

"Yes, I just closed it."

"You lovely boy, pull your tongue in," she instructs the dog, because he's been letting it loll.

Raphael pulls in his tongue, and she sets to work on his front teeth as just the tip of his tail wags.

The caffeine has not yet begun to kick in, and I have no more energy to pursue the issue of the door. "Up at the service station, there's this mechanic named Donny. He has two personalities, and the second one is likely to use a lug wrench in ways its manufacturer never intended. If he comes knocking at your door, don't let him in."

"I don't intend to let anyone in but you."

"That waitress you spoke to when you rented the cottages—"

"Holly Harmony."

"Was she . . . normal?"

"She was lovely, friendly, and efficient."

"She didn't do anything strange?"

"What do you mean?"

"I don't know. Like . . . she didn't pluck a fly out of the air and eat it or anything?"

"What a curious thing to ask."

"Did she?"

"No. Of course not."

"Did she keep almost breaking into tears?"

"Not at all. She had the sweetest smile."

"Maybe she smiled too much?"

"It isn't possible to smile too much, odd one."

"Did you ever see the Joker in *Batman*?"

Finished with Raphael's dental hygiene, Annamaria puts the toothbrush aside and uses the hand towel to mop his face once more. The retriever grins like the Joker.

As she picks up a grooming comb and begins to work on Raphael's silky coat, she says, "The little finger on her right hand ended between the second and third knuckles."

"Who? The waitress? Holly? You said she was normal."

"There's nothing abnormal about losing part of a finger in an accident. It's not in the same category as eating a fly."

"Did you ask her how it happened?"

"Of course not. That would have been rude. The little finger on her *left* hand ends between the first and second knuckles. It's just a stump."

"Wait, wait, wait. Two chopped little fingers is *definitely* abnormal."

"Both injuries could have happened in the same accident."

"Yeah, of course, you're right. She could have been juggling a meat cleaver in each hand when she fell off the unicycle."

"Sarcasm doesn't become you, young man."

I don't know why her mild disapproval stings, but it does.

As though he understands that I have been gently reprimanded, Raphael stops grinning. He favors me with a stern look, as though he suspects that if I'm capable of being sarcastic with Annamaria, I might be the kind of guy who sneaks biscuits from the dog-treat jar and eats them himself.

I say, "Donny the mechanic has a huge scar across his face."

"Did you ask *him* how it happened?" Annamaria inquires.

"I would have, but then Sweet Donny became Angry Donny, and I thought if I asked, he might demonstrate on *my* face."

"Well, I'm pleased that you're making progress."

"If this is the rate of progress I can expect, we better rent the cottages by the year."

As she makes long, easy strokes with the comb, the teeth snare loose hairs from the dog's glorious coat. "You haven't already stopped snooping for the night, have you?"

"No, ma'am. I've just begun to snoop."

"Then I'm sure you'll get to the truth of things shortly."

Raphael decides to forgive me. He grins at me once more, and in response to the tender grooming that he's receiving, he lets out a sound of pure bliss—part sigh, part purr, part whimper of delight.

"You sure do have a way with dogs, ma'am."

"If they know you love them, you'll always have their trust and devotion."

Her words remind me of Stormy, the way we were with each other, our love and trust and devotion. I say, "People are like that, too."

"Some people. Generally speaking, however, people are more problematic than dogs."

"The bad ones, of course."

"The bad ones, the ones adrift between good and bad, and some of the good ones. Even being loved profoundly and forever doesn't necessarily inspire devotion in them."

"That's something to think about."

"I'm sure you've thought about it often, Oddie."

"Well, I'm off to snoop some more," I declare, turning toward the door, but then I don't move.

After combing the long, lush fringe of fur on the dog's left foreleg, which retriever aficionados call feathers, Annamaria says, "What is it?"

"The door is closed."

"To keep out the mercurial mechanic, Donny, about whom you have so effectively warned me."

"It only opens itself when I'm approaching it from outside."

"Your point being—what?"

"I don't know. I'm just saying."

I look at Raphael. Raphael looks at Annamaria.

Annamaria looks at me. I look at the door. It remains closed.

Finally, I take the knob in hand and open the door.

She says, "I knew you could do it."

Gazing out at the night-shrouded motor court, where the trees discreetly shiver, I dread the bloodshed that I suspect I will be required to commit. "There's no real harmony in Harmony Corner."

She says, "But there's a corner in it. Make sure you're not trapped there, young man."

Four

IN CASE I AM BEING WATCHED, I DON'T immediately continue my snooping, but return to my cottage and lock the door behind me.

Not many years ago, nearly 100 percent of people who thought they were being constantly watched were certifiable paranoids. But recently it was revealed that, in the name of public safety, Homeland Security and more than a hundred other local, state, and federal agencies are operating aerial surveillance drones of the kind previously used only on foreign battlefields—at low altitudes outside the authority of air-traffic control. Soon, the bigger worry will not be that, as you walk your dog, you are secretly being watched but that the rapidly proliferating drones will begin colliding with one another and with passenger aircraft,

Odd Interlude   45

and that you'll be killed by the plummeting drone that was monitoring you to be sure that you picked up Fido's poop in a federally approved pet-waste bag.

Having returned to my cottage, I consider switching on the TV to a channel running classic movies, to see if Katharine Hepburn or Cary Grant will suggest that I should sleep. But the caffeine will soon pin my eyelids open, and I suspect that I need to be at least on the brink of nodding off before the invader—whoever or whatever it might be—can access me through the television.

I switch off most of the lights, so that from outside it might appear that I'm finished exploring Harmony Corner and am leaving one lamp aglow as a night-light. Sitting on the edge of the bed, I eat a candy bar.

One of the benefits of living in almost constant jeopardy is that I don't need to worry about things like cholesterol and tooth decay. I'm sure to be killed long before my arteries can be closed by plaque. As for dental cavities, I tend instead to lose my teeth in violent confrontations. Not yet twenty-two, I already have seven teeth that are man-made implants.

I eat the second candy bar. Soon, thanks to all the sugar and caffeine, I should be so wired that I'll be able to receive the nearest tower-of-power radio broadcast through the titanium pins that lock those seven artificial teeth into my jawbone. I hope it won't be a greatest-hits station specializing in seventies disco tunes.

I switch off the last lamp, which is on a nightstand.

Beyond the bed, in the back wall of the cottage, one crank-operated casement window offers a view of the night woods. The two panes open inward to provide fresh air, and a screen keeps out moths and other pests. The screen is spring-loaded from the top and easily removed. From outside, I reinstall it with little noise.

The final aspect of my sixth sense is what Stormy called psychic magnetism. If I need to find someone whose where-abouts I do not know, I keep his name at the forefront of my thoughts and his face in my mind's eye. Then I walk or bicycle, or drive, with no route intended, going where whim takes me, although in fact I am being drawn toward the needed person by an uncanny intuition. Usually within half an hour, often faster, I locate the one I seek.

Psychic magnetism also works—although less well—when I'm searching for an inanimate object, and occasionally even when I'm searching for a place that I can name only by its function. For instance, in this case, wandering behind the arc of cottages and through the moonlit woods, I keep in mind the word *lair*.

A unique Presence is at work in Harmony Corner, someone or something that can travel by television and push a drowsy man into deep sleep, entering his dreams with the expectation that, while he sleeps, his lifetime of memories can be read, his mind searched as easily as a burglar might ransack a house for valuables. That entity, human or otherwise, must have a physical form, for in my experience no spirit possesses such powers. This creature resides somewhere, and considering its seemingly predatory nature, where it resides is best described as a lair rather than a home.

Soon I arrive at the end of the woods, beyond which the grassy land descends in pale, gentle waves toward the shore, perhaps three hundred yards distant. Incoming from the west, dark waves of a more transitory nature ceaselessly disassemble themselves on the sand. The declining moon silvers the knee-high grass, the beach, and the foam into which the breaking waves dissolve.

I am overlooking a cove. On the highlands to the north are the lights of the service station and the diner. A black ribbon, perhaps a lane of pavement, unspools from behind the diner, through the moon-frosted grass, diagonally over the descending series of slopes and along the vales, to a cluster of buildings just above the beach, near the southern end of the cove.

They appear to be seven houses, one larger than the other six, but all of generous size. In two of the structures, a few windows glow with lamplight, but five houses are dark.

If the extended Harmony family, including sons-in-law and daughters-in-law, staff the enterprises just off the coast highway, twenty-four hours a day, seven days a week, they will live nearby. This must be their private little enclave of homes, a picturesque and privileged place to live, though somewhat remote.

Although this is a mild January, snakes are most likely not as active in these meadows as they will be in warmer seasons, and especially not in the coolness of the night. I particularly dislike snakes. I was once locked overnight in a serpentarium where many specimens had been released from their glass viewing enclosures. If they had offered me apples from the tree of knowledge, I might have hoped to cope with that, but they wanted only to inject me with their venom, denying me the chance to undo the world's disastrous history.

I wade down through the sloping meadows, grass to my knees, until I come, unbitten by lurking serpents and unscathed by plummeting drones, to the blacktop lane, which I follow toward the houses.

They are charming Victorian homes graced with generous porches and decorative millwork—some call it gingerbread—exuberantly applied. In the moonlight, they all appear to be in the Gothic Revival style: asymmetrical, irregular massings with steeply pitched roofs that include dormer windows, other windows surmounted by Gothic arches, and elaborately trimmed gables.

Six houses stand side by side on big lots, and the

seventh—which is also the largest—presides over the others from a hilltop, thirty feet above them and a hundred feet behind. Lights are on in a second-floor room of the dominant residence, and also in several rooms on the ground floor in the last of the six front-row dwellings.

At first I feel pulled toward that last house on the lane. As I reach it, however, I find myself continuing past the end of the pavement and down a slope, along a rutted dirt track on which broken seashells crunch and rattle underfoot.

The beach is shallow, bordered by a ten-foot bank overgrown with brush, perhaps wild Olearia. About three feet high, the waves crest late, collapsing abruptly with a low rumble, as if slumbering dragons are grumbling in their sleep.

Thirty feet to the north, movement catches my eye. Alert to my arrival, someone drops to a crouch on the sand.

Reaching under my sweatshirt, I draw the pistol from the small of my back.

I raise my voice to outspeak the sea. "Who's there?"

The figure springs up and sprints to the overgrown embankment. It's slight, about four and a half feet tall, a child, most likely a girl. A flag of long pale hair flutters briefly in the moonlight, and then she disappears against the dark backdrop of brush.

Intuition tells me that if she is not the one I have set

out to find, she is nevertheless key to discovering the truth of things in Harmony Corner.

I angle toward the embankment as I hurry north. Earlier, the purling waves must have reached within a foot of the brush, because now that high tide has passed, the narrow strip between the surf line and the enshrouded slope is still damp and firmly compacted.

After I have gone perhaps a hundred feet without catching sight of my quarry, I realize that I have passed her by. I turn back and make my way south, studying the dark hillside for some path by which she might have ascended through the vegetation.

Instead of a trail, I discover the dark mouth of a culvert that I hadn't noticed in my rush to pursue the girl. It's immense, perhaps six feet in diameter, set in the embankment and overhung in part by vines.

Backlit as I am by the westering moon, I assume that she can see me. "I don't mean you any harm," I assure her.

When she doesn't answer, I push through the straggled vines and take two steps into the enormous concrete drainpipe. I now must be a somewhat less defined silhouette to her, but she remains invisible to me. She might be within arm's reach or a hundred feet away.

I hold my breath and listen for her breathing, but the rumbling pulse of the sea becomes an encircling susurration in the pipe, sliding around and around the curved walls. I can't hear anything as subtle as a child's respiration—or her stealthy footsteps if she is approaching me through the blind-black tunnel.

Considering that she is a young girl and that I am a grown man unknown to her, she will surely retreat farther into the pipe as I advance, rather than attempt to bowl me off my feet and escape—unless she is feral or dangerously psychotic, or both.

Years of violent encounters and supernatural experiences have ripened the fruits on the tree of my imagination past the point of wholesomeness. A few steps farther into the pipe, I am halted by a mental image of a blond girl: eyes glittering feverishly, lips peeled in a snarl, perfect matched-pearl teeth, between several of which are stuck shreds of bloody meat, the flesh of something she has eaten raw. She's got a huge two-tined fork in one hand and a wicked carving knife in the other, eager to slice my abdomen as if it were a turkey.

This is not a psychic vision, merely a boogeygirl sparked into existence by the rubbing together of my frayed nerves. As ridiculous as this fear might be, it nevertheless reminds me that I would be foolish, pistol or not, to proceed farther in such absolute darkness.

"I'm sorry if I've frightened you."

She abides in silence.

Reason having dismissed my imagined psychopathic

child, I speak to the real one. "I know something is very wrong in Harmony Corner."

The revelation of my knowledge fails to charm the girl into conversation.

"I've come to help."

The claim of noble intent I've just made embarrasses me, because it seems boastful, as if I believe that the people of Harmony Corner have been waiting for none but me and, now that I am here, can rest assured that I will set right all wrongs and bring justice to the unjust.

My sixth sense is peculiar but humble. I am no superhero. In fact, I screw up sometimes, and people die when I want desperately to save them. Indeed, my primary strange talent, the ability to see the spirits of the lingering dead, has not come into play here, and I am left with only uncannily sharp intuition, psychic magnetism, a ghost dog that keeps wandering off somewhere, and an appreciation for the role that absurdity plays in our lives. If Superman lost his ability to fly, his strength, his X-ray vision, his imperviousness to blades and bullets, and was left only with his costume and his confidence, he would be of more help to the Harmony family than I am likely to be.

"I'm leaving now," I inform the darkness, my voice echoing hollowly along the curves of concrete. "I hope you're not afraid of me. I'm not afraid of you. I only want to be your friend."

I am beginning to wonder if I might be alone. Perhaps the figure I'd seen had found a way through the brush and up the embankment, in which case the timid girl to whom I now spoke was as imaginary as the homicidal one with the carving knife.

As I have learned before, it is possible to feel as foolish when alone as when one's lapse in judgment or behavior is witnessed by an astonished crowd.

To avoid feeling even sillier, I decide not to exit the pipe backward, but instead to turn and walk out with no concern about who might be at my back. With the first step, my imagination conjures a knife arcing through the darkness, and by my third step, I expect the point of the weapon to stab past my left shoulder blade and into my heart.

I exit the drainpipe without being wounded, turn left on the beach, and walk away with the increasing conviction that, whatever kind of movie I'm in, it's not a slasher film. When I reach the rutted track littered with broken shells, I look back, but the girl—if it had been a girl—is nowhere to be seen.

Returning to the blacktop lane and the last of the seven houses, where lamplight brightens a couple of ground-floor rooms, I decide to reconnoiter window-to-window. As I climb the front steps with catlike stealth and mouselike caution, a woman says, "What do you want?"

Pistol still in hand, I hold it down at my side, counting on the gloom to conceal it. At the top of the steps, I see what seem to be four wicker chairs with cushions, all in a row on the porch. The woman sits in the third of them, barely revealed by the glow that emanates from the curtained window behind her. I smell the coffee then, and I can see her just well enough to discern that she holds a mug in both hands.

"I want to help," I tell her.

"Help what?"

"All of you."

"What makes you think we need help?"

"Donny's scarred face. Holly's amputated fingers."

She drinks her coffee.

"And a thing that almost happened to me as I drank a beer and watched TV."

Still she does not reply.

The rhythmic rumble of the surf is hushed from here.

Finally she says, "We've been warned about you."

"Warned by whom?"

Instead of answering, she says, "We've been warned to avoid you . . . and we think we know why."

In the west, the moon is as round as the face of a pocket watch, and in this exceptionally clear sky, it seems to have a fob of stars.

The dawn is still more than an hour from the eastern horizon. I don't know why, but I think that getting one of them to speak frankly will be easier in the dark.

She says, "I'll be punished if I tell you anything. Punished severely."

Had she already decided not to speak with me, she would have no need to suggest that she will pay dearly for doing so. She simply would tell me to go away.

She needs a reason to take the risk, and I think that I know what might motivate her. "Is that your daughter I saw on the beach?"

The woman's eyes glisten faintly with ambient light.

I take the first seat, leaving an empty chair between us, and hold the pistol in my lap.

With less dismay than I ought to feel, I seek to manipulate her. "Is your daughter scarred yet? Does she still have all her fingers? Has she been punished severely?"

"You don't need to do that."

"Do what, ma'am?"

"Push me so hard."

"I'm sorry."

"What are you?" she asks. "Who do you work for?"

"I'm an agent, ma'am, but I can't say of what."

That is true enough. I could tell her what I'm *not* an agent of: the FBI, the CIA, the BATF. . . . The office that I hold comes without a badge or a paycheck, and although it seems to me that my gift makes me the agent of some higher power, I can't prove it and dare not say as much for fear of being thought delusional.

Strangely emotionless considering her words, she says, "Jolie, my daughter, is twelve. She's smart and strong and good. And she's going to be killed."

"What makes you think so?"

"Because she's too beautiful to live."

Five

THE WOMAN'S NAME IS ARDYS, THE WIFE OF William Harmony, whose parents created Harmony Corner.

A time existed, she says, when life here was as ideal as it can be anywhere. They enjoyed the grace of a close-knit family and the blessing of a sustaining enterprise in which they labored together, without conflict, perhaps much as pioneer families of another era worked a plot of land, producing together what they needed to survive and producing, at the same time, a history of accomplishment and shared experience that bound them together in the best of ways.

From the start of the Corner, the family's children have been homeschooled, and both children and adults have preferred to spend most of their leisure time fishing in this cove, sunning on this beach, walking in these meadowy hills. There were field trips for the school-age kids, of course, and vacations beyond the boundaries of their property—until five years previously. Then Harmony Corner became for them a prison.

She recounts that much in a calm voice so quiet that, at times, I lean sideways in my chair to be sure of hearing every word. She allows herself none of the grief in advance of loss that you might expect if she really believes that young Jolie, as punishment for her beauty, will be killed. Neither does a note of fear enter her voice, and I suspect she must speak without emotion or otherwise entirely lose the self-control that is required to speak to me at all.

Literally a prison, she says. No one any longer vacations off these grounds. No day trips are taken. Long-time friendships with people outside the family have been terminated, often with a rudeness and pretended anger that will ensure that the former friends make no attempt to patch things up. Only one of them at a time may leave the property, and then only to conduct banking or a limited number of other tasks. They no longer go shopping for anything; what they need must be ordered by phone and delivered.

Although her manner and her tone remain matter-of-fact, her voice is haunting, because she is a haunted woman. The revelation toward which she is leading me has bound her spirit but not yet broken it. I sense in her a despondency that is an incapacity for the current exercise of hope, a despondency that arises when resistance to some adversity has long proved futile. But she does not seem to have fallen all the way into the settled hopelessness of despair.

I'm surprised, therefore, when she stops speaking. When I press her to continue, she remains silent, staring solemnly at the dark sea as if it calls to her to drown herself in its cold waters.

Waiting is one of the things that human beings cannot do well, though it is one of the essential things we must do successfully if we are to know happiness. We are impatient for the future and try to craft it with our own powers, but the future will come as it comes and will not be hurried. If we are good at waiting, we discover that what we wanted of the future, in our impatience, is no longer what we want, that waiting has brought wisdom. I have become good at waiting, as I wait to see what action or sacrifice is wanted of me, wait to discover where I must go next, and wait for the day when the fortune-teller's promise will be fulfilled. Hope, love, and faith are in the waiting.

After a few minutes, Ardys says, "For a moment, I thought I felt it opening."

"What?"

"The door. My own private door. How do I tell you more when I'm afraid that mentioning his name or describing him might bring him to me before I can explain our plight?"

When she falls silent again, I recall this: "They say you should never speak the devil's name because next thing you know, you'll hear his footsteps on the stairs."

"At least there are ways of dealing with the devil," she says, implying that there may be no way to deal with her nameless enemy.

As I wait for her to continue and as she waits to find a route to her truth that will be safe, the darkness beyond the porch railing seems vast, seems to be washing in around us as the black sea washes to the nearby shore. Night itself is the sea of all seas, reaching to the farthest end of the universe, the moon and every planet and every star afloat in it. Here in this waiting moment, I almost feel that this house and the other six houses, the distant diner and service station—the lights of which seem like ship lights—are being lifted and turned in the night, in danger of coming loose of their moorings.

Having found a way to approach her truth indirectly, without mentioning the devil's name, Ardys says, "You've met Donny. You saw his scar. He transgressed, and that was his punishment. He thought that if he was sufficiently deceitful and quick enough, he would win our freedom with a knife. Instead, he turned it upon himself and slashed his own face."

I thought I must have misunderstood. "He did that to himself?"

She holds up a hand as if to say *Wait*. She sets aside her coffee mug. She lays her arms on the arms of the chair, but there is nothing relaxed about her posture. "If I am too specific . . . if I explain why he would do such a thing to himself, then I will say what I must not say, the thing that will be heard and that will summon to us what must not be summoned."

My mention of the devil seems more apt by the moment, for there is in what she just said something that reminds me of the cadences of Scripture.

"Donny might have died if his death had been wanted, but what was wanted was his suffering. Though he was bleeding profusely and in terrible pain, he remained calm. Though his speech was impeded by his cut lips, he told us to tie him down to a kitchen table and to put a folded cloth in his mouth to stifle the screams that would shortly come and to ensure that he would not bite his tongue."

She continues speaking in a quiet voice from which all drama and most inflection are edited, and it is this self-control, which takes such a great effort of will, that lends credence to her incredible story. Her hands have closed into tightly clenched fists.

"His wife, Denise, who is screaming and near collapse, seems suddenly to collect herself—just as Donny at last begins to scream. She tells us what she will need to staunch the bleeding, sterilize the wound as best she can, and sew it up. You see, she must share in Donny's punishment by being the instrument that ensures his permanent disfigurement, which a first-rate surgeon might have minimized. There will be nerve damage and numbness. And every time she looks at him for the rest of their lives, she will in part blame herself for not being able to resist . . . to resist being used in this fashion. We know that if we fail to assist her, any one of us might be the next to slash his own face. We assist. She closes the wound."

Ardys's fists unclench, and she lowers her head. She has about her an air of exhaustion, as if analyzing her words before speaking them, with an ear for those that might summon the Presence that she fears, has drained both her physical and mental reserves.

Less than an hour of darkness remains, yet the night seems to be rising, submerging the hills, lifting the houses out of anchorage to set them adrift. This perception is nothing more than a reflection of my state of mind; a change in my conception of reality, of what's possible or not, is what has actually for a moment unmoored me.

If I understand Ardys, then the Presence that entered my dream and tried to explore the archives of my memory is more than a reader. It is in their case a *controller* of great power and greater cruelty, a tyrannical puppeteer.

Beginning five years earlier, it has made of Harmony Corner not precisely a prison and not in scope an empire, but a pocket universe akin to a primitive island on which a god carved of stone demands absolute obedience, with the difference that *this* false deity is capable of brutally enforcing its commands. It entered rebellious Donny and forced him to mutilate himself, and thereafter it entered Denise and, using her hands, made sure that Donny's face would always testify to the dire consequence of disobedience.

Earlier, when Sweet Donny became Angry Donny, the Presence must have entered him and taken control. I had suddenly been talking not to the mechanic's second and less appealing personality, but instead to another individual entirely, the puppetmaster.

The service station had no television, and Donny was wide awake when he was abruptly possessed. My understanding of how the Presence travels and how it takes up tenancy in another's mind is incomplete. Watching the boob tube might not be an invitation to this particular damnation, after all—though it's still not a wise idea to spend a lot of time watching reality-TV shows about celebrity families living in the wild with gorillas.

I realize, too, that by "my own private door" Ardys means the door to her mind. For a moment, she thought that she felt it opening.

They live in unceasing expectation of being invaded, controlled. How they have held fast to their sanity for five years is beyond my comprehension.

Although I assume Ardys has said as much as she dares to say, she raises her head and continues, speaking softly and in a voice that might seem weary if I didn't know the effort required of her to make it sound so. "My sister-in-law, Laura, is a Harmony, but her married name is Jorgenson. She and Steve, her husband, have three children. The middle one was a boy named Maxwell. We called him Maxy."

I am sobered by her determination to maintain a voice without dramatic emphasis and, presumably, also to repress internally the emotions that these revelations should inflame. Her effort suggests that on some level the Presence is always aware of the general mood of each of the subjects in its little kingdom. Perhaps it's alerted to a possibility of disobedience when one of them becomes a bit too agitated emotionally, in much the way that our nation's security forces employ computers to monitor millions of phone calls, not listening to every exchange but scanning for certain combinations of words that might identify a conversation between two terrorists.

"Maxy was always exceptional-looking. A pretty baby, then a beautiful toddler. More handsome year by year. He was six when things changed. He was eight when we learned there is a degree of beauty that, if exceeded, inspires envy and requires the removal of the one whose appearance causes offense."

Her ability to speak of child murder with such bland words and in such a dispassionate tone indicates that in the three years since the killing of Maxy, she has developed and refined techniques of self-possession that I could never match. She is eerily composed, all excited feeling subdued, for this is what she must do to survive—and now to save her daughter.

She says, "There's a short story by Shirley Jackson, 'The Lottery,' which concerns a ritual stoning. Everyone in the town must participate so that something outrageous and morally repugnant may seem normal, essential to public order, and a moment of community bonding. Those who participate in that lottery do so voluntarily. When someone too beautiful had to be removed from the Corner, everyone participated, one after the other, including Maxy himself, but none voluntarily."

The horrific scene she suggests with such restraint chills me as much as anything ever has.

I am inexpressibly grateful that I am invulnerable to the power of this mysterious Presence. But then I pray that I am indeed not vulnerable, because perhaps on second try the puppetmaster will find a way to open my own private door.

Speaking now in a whisper, Ardys says, "Here, mere stones are considered uninspired. More imagination is employed. And unlike in the Jackson story, the sacrifice is not performed efficiently but with an intention to prolong the event as you might want to see a good ball game go into several extra innings to increase the drama and the ultimate satisfaction."

My palms are damp. I blot them on my jeans before picking up the pistol from my lap.

"In three years, there has not been another whose appearance has caused such offense," Ardys informs me. "Until recently. Members of our family have begun expressing envy of my daughter's growing beauty, both to her and to me. Of course I mean this envy has been expressed by another for whom they are forced to speak."

I have a hundred questions, but before I can pose one, Ardys gets up from the chair and asks that I come with her.

She opens the front door and leads me inside.

For a moment, I look back warily at the shadowed porch and the deeper gloom beyond. When I close the door, I turn the deadbolt, for it seems that the night itself might rise like a rough beast and slouch across the threshold in our wake.

I follow her along the hallway to the immaculate kitchen. In my experience, everything in Harmony Corner is spotless. Hard work must be essential to relieve their minds from continuous morbid consideration of their desperate situation. Focusing intently on what they *can* control—like the cleanliness of their homes and enterprises—must be one of the few ways they can keep aglow the embers of hope.

In the kitchen light, I discover that Ardys Harmony is lovely. Perhaps in her late thirties, she has a complexion as clear as light, and her eyes are the color of crème de menthe, darker green than I would have thought any eyes could be. Her otherwise perfect skin is marked by crow's-feet, but those tiny wrinkles seem to me to be evidence not of aging but instead of the courage and the steel willpower with which she faces each day in the Corner, as even now her eyes are squinted and her mouth tightly set with determination.

She draws me to the sink, above which is a window that frames a view of the larger house on the hill behind this one. As earlier, lamplight brightens some of the second-floor windows in that imposing residence.

"My husband's parents bought this property in a fore-closure sale in 1955. It was dilapidated. They revitalized the businesses, turned failure into success, and built additional houses as their children got married and the family grew. They lived in the hilltop house until they died, both of them nine years ago. Bill and I lived up there four years—until everything changed. Five years now, we've lived down here."

Without directly telling me that their controller and tormentor can be found in the highest of the seven houses, without mentioning a name or providing a description, without putting her request into words that might draw unwanted attention, she nevertheless conveys to me by her eyes and her expression what she hopes I might achieve. Maybe I, immune to the powers of the Presence, will be able to enter its lair undetected and kill it. I understand what she wants of me as clearly as if I could read minds.

If the Presence is alone and the Harmonys are many, and if it can control only one person at a time—as the story of Donny's cut and Denise's sewing up of his wound seems to indicate—then surely sometime in five years, they might have found a way to overwhelm their enemy. I don't have enough information, however, to understand their long enslavement or to calculate the odds of my succeeding at the task she hopes that I will undertake.

The need to speak somewhat indirectly of these things and in a subdued manner complicates my information gathering. I ask, "Is it a man I'm looking for or something else?"

She turns from the window. "This line of talk is inadvisable."

I persist: "A man?"

"Yes and no."

"What does that mean?"

She shakes her head. She dares not say, for fear the words she would need to describe my quarry might alert him to the fact that we are conspiring against him. This suggests that once he has taken control of someone, even after he departs that person, the two of them remain linked at all times, at least tenuously.

"He's only one, I assume."

"Yes."

She looks at the pistol in my hand.

I ask, "Will this be enough to do the job?"

Her expression is bleak. "I don't know."

As I consider how best to word certain other questions without setting off a psychic alarm in the mind of the Presence, I ask if I may have a drink of water.

She plucks a bottle of Niagara from the refrigerator, and as I put down the pistol on the dinette table, I assure her that I don't need a glass.

For a man closing in on twenty-four hours without sleep, after a long day of exhausting action, too much caffeine is as problematic as too little. Drowsiness and the lack of focus that it promotes could be the death of me, although so could the edginess and the tendency to overreact that come with an overdose of stimulants. But Mountain Dew, candy bars, and a pair of NoDoz have not yet quite cleared the sandman's dust from my eyes. I swallow one more caffeine tablet.

As I put down the water, Ardys comes to me and takes one of my hands in both of hers. Her eyes seem to express desperation, and her look is beseeching.

Something about her stare, perhaps the intensity of it, makes me uneasy. Because my life is marbled with the supernatural, I'm creeped out frequently enough to be familiar with the feeling that something is crawling on the nape of my neck. This time, however, before I can smooth down those fine hairs with my free hand, I realize that the crawling isn't on my neck but *inside* my skull.

As I slam my own private door, rejecting what has sought to enter, Ardys says, "Have you figured out how to express it better, Harry?"

"Express what?"

"The analogy with the porpoise and the prairie dog."

Alarmed, I twist my hand free of hers.

The form of Jolie's mother still stands before me, and surely the substance of her—mind and soul—still inhabits the body even if she is no longer in control of it. The Presence and I are face-to-face, as last we were when it challenged me through Donny, and this time its true countenance is concealed by the Ardys mask. Her skin remains clear and radiant, but her expression of utter contempt is one that I doubt is familiar to that lovely

visage. Those dark-green eyes are as striking as they were
before, like the eyes of a woman in some magic-saturated
Celtic myth, but they are no longer haunted or sad, or
beseeching; they seem to radiate a palpable, inhuman fury.

I snatch the gun from the table.

She says, "Who are you really, Harry Potter?"

"Lex Luthor," I admit. "That's why I had to change my
name. The thousandth time someone asked me why I hated
Superman, I started wishing my name was just about
anything else, even Fidel Castro."

"You are the first of your kind I've ever encountered."

"What kind is that?" I wonder.

"Inaccessible. I possess everyone who sleeps in the motor
court, roam their memories, and embed recurrent night-
mares that will destroy their sleep for weeks after I've
departed them."

"I'd prefer a free continental breakfast."

Not stiffly, like a zombie, but with her usual grace,
she walks—almost seems to glide—to the counter beside
the cooktop and opens a drawer. "Sometimes I seize
control of motor-court guests while they're awake—use
a husband to brutalize a wife or use a wife to tell her
husband lies about infidelities that I imagine for her in
delicious detail."

Ardys stares into the drawer.

"When they leave," the Presence says through her,

"they're beyond my control, but what I've done will have a lasting effect."

"Why? What's the point?"

Ardys looks up from the drawer. "Because I can. Because I want to. Because I will."

"That's a tidy little moral vacuum."

Obeying the beast that rides her, Ardys withdraws a meat cleaver from the drawer. In her voice, the hidden demon says, "Not a vacuum. A black hole. Nothing escapes me."

I suggest, "Delusions of grandeur."

Raising the cleaver, Ardys approaches the dinette table, which stands between us. "You're a fool."

"Yeah? Well, you're a narcissist."

I find it dismaying that we never quite outgrow the schoolyard and the puerile behavior thereof. Even this puppetmaster, with almost godlike power over those it controls, feels the need to belittle me with childish insults, and I feel obliged to respond in kind.

Through Ardys, it says, "You're dead, shitface."

"Yeah? Well, you're probably ugly as hell."

"Not when I'm in this bitch."

"I'd rather be dead than as ugly as you."

"You're ugly enough, shitface."

I reply, "Sticks and stones."

She starts around the table.

I circle in the other direction, taking a two-hand grip on the pistol and aiming it point-blank at her chest.

"You won't shoot her," the Presence says.

"I killed a woman earlier tonight."

"Liar."

"Freak."

"Killing the bitch won't kill me."

"But you'll have to find another host. By then I'll be out of the house, and you won't know where to look for me."

She throws the cleaver.

My paranormal ability includes occasional prophetic dreams but not, darn it, glimpses of the future while I'm awake, which would be really, really helpful in moments like this.

I don't expect her to throw it, I haven't time to dodge, the blade whooshes past my face close enough to shave me if I had a beard, and chops into the cabinetry behind me, splitting the raised panel on an upper door.

The puppeteer is probably limited to the physical capabilities of whatever host it inhabits. I am maybe fifteen years younger than Ardys, stronger, with longer legs. The Presence is right, I won't kill Ardys, she's innocent, a victim, and now as she returns to the knife drawer, there's nothing I can do but split in the figurative sense before her rider uses her to split me literally.

I race along the hallway, reaching the foyer just as the front door opens and a tall, husky guy halts on the threshold, startled to see me. He must be the husband, William Harmony. I say, "Hi, Bill," hoping he'll politely step out of the way, but even as I speak, his expression hardens, and he says, "Shitface," which either means that the insult is so appropriate that it's the first thing people think to say when catching sight of me *or* the Presence has flipped out of Ardys and into her spouse.

Although I don't know Bill as well as I know Ardys, I don't want to shoot this innocent, either. Call me prissy. If I retreat to the kitchen, the puppeteer will flip out of Bill and into Ardys once more, and she'll have a carving knife or a butcher knife, or a battery-powered electric knife, or a chain saw if they happen to keep one in the kitchen. Bill is wearing a sailor's cap, which is appropriate, because his neck is as thick as a wharf post, his hands look as big as anchors, and his chest is as wide as the prow of a ship. There's no way that I can go through him, which leaves me no choice but to sprint up the nearby staircase to the second floor.

Six

I AM PERPETUALLY—SOMETIMES DARKLY—
amused by the workings of my mind, which can often seem
less rational than I would like to believe they are. The
human brain is by far the most complex object known to
exist in the entire universe, containing more neurons than
there are billions of stars in the Milky Way. The brain and
the mind are very different things, and the latter is as
mysterious as the former is complex. The brain is a
machine, and the mind is a ghost within it. The origins of
self-awareness and how the mind is able to perceive,
analyze, and imagine are supposedly explained by numerous
schools of psychology, although in fact they study only
behavior through the gathering and the analysis of statis-
tics. The *why* of the mind's existence and the *how* of its

profound capacity to reason—especially its penchant for moral reasoning—will by their very nature remain as mysterious as whatever lies outside of time.

As I race up the stairs to the second floor, intent upon not falling into the hands of the possessed Bill Harmony, who looks like he has the strength to break me apart as easily as I might break in half a breadstick, I am afraid of dying—and therefore failing to protect Annamaria as I promised—and at the same time I am mildly embarrassed by the impropriety of dashing pell-mell toward the more private portion of their residence, into which I haven't been invited.

I hear myself saying, "Sorry, sorry, sorry," as I ascend the stairs, which seems absurd, considering that my trespass is a far lesser offense than the puppetmaster's intention to use Mr. Harmony to bash my brains out. On the other hand, I think it speaks well of human beings that we are capable of recognizing when we've committed an impropriety even while we're in a desperate fight for survival. I've read that in the worst Nazi and Soviet slave-labor camps, where never enough food was provided to inmates, the stronger prisoners nearly always shared rations equitably with weaker ones, recognizing that the survival instinct does not entirely excuse us from the need to be charitable. Not all human competition has to be as brutal as that on the Food Network's *Cupcake Wars*.

At the head of the stairs, as I hear Mr. Harmony thundering up the two flights behind me, I discover that the hallway leads right and left. I turn left, trusting my intuition, which unfortunately isn't 100 percent reliable.

Out of a room to my right, a boy of about fifteen, barechested and barefoot, wearing pajama bottoms, erupts as if catapulted, slams into me, drives me into the wall, and reveals himself to be possessed when he says, "Shitface."

Although the impact knocks the wind out of me, although I drop the pistol, although the boy's sour breath reeks of garlic from the previous night's dinner, and although I am beginning to be offended by the unnecessary repetition of that insult to my appearance, I am nevertheless impressed by the puppeteer's ability to switch from host to host in what seems like the blink of an eye. Cool. Terrifying, yes, but definitely cool.

As I drive one knee hard into the boy's crotch, I say, "Sorry, sorry, sorry," which I mean even more sincerely than the regret I expressed for violating the sanctity of their second floor. He collapses into the fetal position with a wordless groan that would most accurately be pronounced "urrrrlll," and I assure him that although he feels that he is dying, he will live.

Mr. Harmony is standing at the head of the stairs, looking confused. But then his face hardens into a gargoyle snarl as the Presence invades him.

After scooping up the pistol, I bolt across the hall, into the room out of which the boy attacked me. I slam the door. In the knob is a button that engages the latch, but there's no deadbolt.

Mr. Harmony tries the door, violently rattling the knob, just as I brace it with a straight-backed chair snared from a nearby desk. Even though the animal that Mr. Harmony most reminds me of is a rhinoceros, this trick should hold him off for a couple of minutes.

At the double-hung eight-pane window, I pull open the draperies, see a porch roof beyond, and disengage the latch. I can't raise the inner sash, and I can't lower the outer sash, because the window has been painted shut.

If I were Mr. Daniel Craig, the most recent James Bond, I would quickly kick out the wooden muntins separating the panes in the lower sash, squeeze through the sash without raising it, and be gone. But I am only me, and I've no doubt that a backspray of shattering glass would blind me, while the bristling end of a broken muntin would pierce one calf or the other, gouge open the peroneal artery, and bleed me dry in 2.1 minutes. Another famous film character, Kermit the Frog, sings a song about how "It's not easy being green," and as true as that might be, it's even less easy being a man who isn't James Bond.

Meanwhile, at the door, Mr. Harmony doesn't bellow like some beast from the African veldt, but he slams his shoulder against the door or kicks it with rhinocerosian fury.

Perhaps sixteen years have passed since I last tried to hide under a bed; and even then I was easily found.

Two additional doors offer the only possibilities. The first leads to a closet in which Mr. Harmony could beat me half to death with his humongous fists and then garrote me with a wire clothes hanger.

The second opens into a bathroom. This door *does* have a deadbolt on the inside. The bathroom features a large frosted-glass window directly above the toilet.

The Victorian tilework offers a field of pale green with here and there hand-painted white baskets overflowing with roses, all set off with white-and-yellow-checkered trim. It strikes me as too busy, even garish, but in the interest of staying alive, I enter the bath anyway and lock the door behind me.

I put the pistol on the counter beside the sink, disengage the well-lubricated window latch, and find to my surprise that the window is not painted shut. The lower sash slides up easily and stays there without need of a prop. Beyond lies the same porch roof I had seen from the other room.

As events have unfolded since I first went snooping, this has seemed like a night when I would be well-advised not to buy a lottery ticket or play Russian roulette. Although now my luck seems to have changed, I'm still not in a mood to sing Kermit the Frog's other hit song, "Rainbow Connection."

Whether it is the sight of the loo or the excitement of the chase, I am suddenly aware that this evening I have drunk a beer, a can of Mountain Dew, and a bottle of water. Mr. Harmony has not quite yet broken down the bedroom door, so it seems wise to take the time to pee here rather than hurry onward and soon be hampered in my flight by having to run with my thighs pressed together.

With the personal-hygiene vigilance of a responsible short-order cook, I'm washing my hands as the bedroom door at last crashes open. I blot them on my sweatshirt, snatch up the pistol, stand on the closed lid of the toilet, and hastily exit the window onto the roof of the porch.

This is the front-porch roof, under which I sat with Ardys. That was only minutes earlier, but it seems like an hour has passed since she first began to talk to me.

The blush of dawn has not yet touched the eastern horizon. In the west, the moon discreetly retreats beyond the curve of the earth, and it almost seems that the stars, as well, are receding. Second by second, the dark night grows yet darker.

As the demon-ridden Mr. Harmony begins trying to kick down the bathroom door, I cross the sloped roof toward its lowest edge. I leap off, land on the lawn nine feet below without fracturing my ankles, drop, roll, and spring to my feet.

For an instant, I feel like a prince of derring-do, swashbuckler sans sword. Honest pride can slide quickly into vanity, however, and then into vainglory, and when in the manner of a musketeer you take a bow with a flourish of your feathered hat, you're likely to raise your head into the downswing of a villain's hatchet.

I need to get away from the house, but following the blacktop lane up through the hills and vales will surely lead to encounters with possessed members of the Harmony family. I have learned much less about the Presence than I need to know, but I have learned too much to be allowed to live. Through one surrogate or another, it will pursue me relentlessly.

It doesn't have to possess these people to force them to do what it wants. However many Harmonys there might be—six big houses full of them, surely no fewer than thirty, most likely forty or more—the puppeteer can alert them that they are required to guard against my escape. They will obey out of fear that it will flip from one to another of them, disfiguring or killing at random to punish the slightest thought of rebellion. If they love one another, none will flee and allow an unknown number of others to be killed as revenge for he who escapes. Freedom at that price isn't freedom at all, but instead an endless highway of guilt from which perhaps there is no exit but suicide.

They will hunt me down, and I will have to escape with Annamaria or kill them all. I can't bear to kill so many, or even one of them. The ten-round magazine of my pistol contains only seven cartridges. But the shortage of ammunition isn't what prevents me from shooting my way out of the Corner. My past and my future constrain me. By *past* I mean my losses, and by *future* I mean the hope of regaining what has been lost.

With dawn mere minutes away, I can imagine no certain hiding place once morning light floods down through the hills. I need to hide because I need time to think. Before I know what I'm doing, I find myself running across the dark lawn and to the rutted track littered with broken shells.

In the absence of the moon, the ocean is as black as oil and the foam in the breaking surf is now the fungal gray of soap suds in which dirty hands have been washed and washed again. The beach lies starlit, and although the galactic whorls overhead contain as many suns as any shore has grains of sand, this strand is as dim as badly tarnished silver, for our Earth is remote, rotating far from the stars and farther every night.

As I reach the end of the unpaved track, underfoot the shell fragments slide with a sound like the scattered coins of a pirate treasure, and suddenly she rushes past me, having followed me from the house. Without the moon to honor it, her flag of hair is less bright than before, but she is certainly the blond child whom I glimpsed previously, Jolie, daughter of Ardys. If earlier she followed me to the house and then listened to my conversation with her mother on the porch, that explains why, as she passes, she speaks to me as if I am her confirmed conspirator: *"Follow me! Hurry!"*

Seven

JOLIE IS A SHADOW BUT AS QUICK AS LIGHT, and although she gets well ahead of me, she stops to wait at the mouth of the big culvert.

As I arrive there, I hear a man shout not from the beach behind me but perhaps from the houses that stand ten feet above the sea, and another man answers him. Their words are distorted by distance and by being filtered through the sounds of my drumming heart and my rapid breathing, but the meaning of them is nonetheless clear. Those men are in the hunt.

I hear also the engine of some vehicle, perhaps an SUV or a large pickup. From somewhere above and inland, light flares, fades, swells again, and sweeps across the top of the embankment, over our heads, moving north to south. A searchlight. Mounted on a vehicle.

The puppetmaster can marshal its army with shocking speed, because it needs no telephone. And perhaps it doesn't have to possess its subjects one by one to convey the threat that I pose. Maybe it is able to broadcast an instruction to all of them simultaneously, which they are not compelled to obey—as they are compelled when their oppressor enters intimately into one of them—but which they obey nevertheless because the consequences of disobedience are so dire.

Jolie says, "Hold tight to me. We can't risk a light for a while, and the way is very dark."

Her hand is small and delicate in mine, but strong.

We push through the overhanging vines. They are cold ropy creepers that conjure in my mind the strange image of dead snakes dangling from the head of a lifeless Medusa.

As before, the drainage tunnel is as dark as any blind man's world, and it is almost as quiet as a deaf man's life. The rubber soles of our shoes extract little sound from the concrete pipe. The floor is not puddled with water through which we might splash, and no debris has washed here that might crackle underfoot. If vermin share this darkness with us, they are as silent as the rats that slink through dreams.

The air is cool and smells clean. In a drain, even one of this size, especially in the rainy season, which is now, I expect at least the faint scents of mold and spooring fungi, the fetor of occasional stagnant pools skinned with slimy algae, a whiff of lime efflorescing from the concrete. The odorless condition of this realm is no less disorienting than the blackness all around.

We stay to the center, the low point of the curving passage, which means the girl can't be feeling her way along the wall. Yet she proceeds with confidence, never hesitating, walking at an ordinary pace, as if she knows that no obstruction lies ahead, as if all she needs to find her way is the cant of the floor under her feet and a draft so faint that only she can feel it.

I have in the past been in lightless places that were less welcoming than this and fraught with dangers, forced to crawl and explore blindly with my hands. Although this great pipe smells clean and seems to harbor no mortal threats, I find it immeasurably more disturbing than any previous dark place I have known.

Step by step, my nerves become more raw, abraded by the silken darkness, pinched by the silence, and what flutters in my stomach also creeps up and down my spine.

Halting, holding fast to the girl's hand, I ask, "Where are we going?"

She whispers, "*Shhhh. Voices carry in the pipe. If they*

listen at the outlet, maybe they'll hear. Besides, I'm counting steps, so don't confuse me."

I glance back, but the moonless night is still awaiting dawn. Unable to see the vine-straggled outlet, I can't judge how far we might have come.

Jolie continues forward, and I follow.

From the moment we entered, the floor has sloped upward. Now the angle of ascent increases. Soon I sense that this tunnel is curving to the left.

Three disturbing things happen in the next few minutes, two of them in that perfect gloom and the third in weak but welcome light.

First my singular intuition, which if it could smell and see would have the nose of a hunting dog and the eyes of a hawk, tells me with steadily increasing insistence that this tunnel is not what it seems to be. I assume that it must have been constructed to channel torrents of rain from the shoulders of the four-lane highway high above or from a network of open gullies, with the intention of preventing erosion of the coastal hills. But this is not a drain, not a piece of common infrastructure with a public purpose.

Being guided by the girl through the blind and odorless quiet, I perceive a pair of truths about this tunnel, the first being that it proceeds to something other than manholes and drainage grates. Ahead will be found peculiar features, and at some far terminus lies an immense facility of mysterious purpose. These perceptions don't pour into me as a flood of images but as feelings. I am not able to feel them more vividly by concentrating on them, nor can I translate these feelings into clear details. In all its aspects, my psychic gift has always been more powerful than I can comfortably manage but weaker than I wish it were.

The associated truth is that the place to which this passageway ultimately leads is thought to be abandoned but is not entirely so. I have a vague impression of colossal structures, vast rooms that stand empty and others that house exotic machines long unused and corroded. But somewhere in those monumental installations, cocooned by rings of derelict buildings in which nothing moves except fitful drafts and ghosts that are nothing more than bestirred forms of dust, there is a hub of activity. That hub might seem small by comparison to the forsaken architectures that surround it, but my sense is that this secret core is itself large and bunkered, staffed by men and women as busy as the population of any hive.

The second of the three disturbing things that happen in this black passageway, subsequent to the pair of clair-voyantly received truths, is an ominous perception that something pernicious beyond comprehension lies ahead, something unwholesome exceeding all my previous experi-ence of wickedness. A flood tide of apprehension wells and swiftly builds into an almost incapacitating fright, a shrinking, anxious fear that some pure evil looms with all the power of a mile-high tsunami.

I believe—I *know*—that the unknown thing I sense and fear is not here now, but instead waits far ahead, in that fortified hub of which I can *feel* the existence though I cannot see it. This perfect blackness oppresses me, however, and because the girl seems quite at home in it, I am increasingly troubled by the thought that she is so comfortable in the dark because she is *of* the dark, never was the innocent child that I have assumed, but is one with the distant threat toward which she seems to lead me.

She whispers, *"We're coming to a threshold, don't trip,"* and squeezes my hand as if to reassure me.

Her apparent solicitude should steady my nerves a little, but it does not. The perception of some unknown but monumental evil waiting ahead does not relent, in fact intensifies. After hearing the story of young Maxwell's murder by his possessed kin, after seeing lovely Ardys Harmony transformed into a homicidal puppet with a cleaver, I have no reason to dread this unknown menace more than I fear the Presence, the puppetmaster, but my intuition continues to insist.

The promised threshold is perhaps two inches high. My left shoulder brushes what might be a heavy sliding door, and my pistol, clutched in that hand, rings loudly off steel.

Through the sole of one of my shoes, I feel a metal channel inset in the midpoint of the foot-wide threshold.

"The beach is so far away, we can risk it now," Jolie says, letting go of my hand and switching on a small flashlight the size of a Magic Marker.

The flash is welcome although inadequate, the darkness flowing in again behind the beam as it moves, flowing like the cloak of something cowled and hostile, figures of dim light squirming in the stainless-steel walls, as though they are the tortured denizens of some parallel reality separated from ours by a thin, distorting membrane.

The narrow ray reveals that we have left the pipe behind and have entered a rectangular chamber approximately ten feet wide and twenty long. The floor seems to be white ceramic tiles separated not by grout lines but by thin spines of polished steel. All other surfaces are stainless steel.

With the beam, the girl indicates a crowbar and several wood wedges of different sizes, which lie together in a corner. "I had to pry open the doors, and it wasn't easy, I about thought I'd blow out a carotid artery. They were pneumatic once, I think, but there's no power to them now."

The breached darkness is more disturbing than the blinding gloom that preceded it. Even in cramped quarters, absolute blackness allows the mind to imagine a generous space, but here the ceiling is hardly more than seven feet above the floor, and the sheen of the cold steel is sinister.

"What is this place?" I ask.

"Maybe the pipe behind us was just a storm drain a long time ago, before Grandpa even bought the Corner. But someone connected this system to it. Someone weird and up to no good, if you ask me." She plays the light across the walls to the left and right, where the smooth steel is interrupted by double rows of inch-diameter holes. "I've thought about it a lot, and what I figure is this was first of all some kind of escape route. If people used it, they were decontaminated in these rooms—you know, maybe because of bacteria and viruses. Maybe. I don't know. Feels right. But if you weren't people, if you were anything else and you got this far, they trapped you here and instead of pumping in germ-killing mist or whatever, they instead pumped poison gas into the room."

" 'If you were anything else'? What anything?"

Before the girl can respond, a rumbling arises, not unlike the subterranean roar of certain earthquakes. It seems to come from overhead, however, and as it grows louder, I look uneasily at the ceiling.

"Probably an eighteen-wheeler," Jolie says. "We're under the Coast Highway here, beyond the Corner."

She leads the way to the end of the room, where four steps ascend to a second threshold. Here she has pried open another set of steel doors. Beyond lies a chamber identical to the first.

She plays the light over the architrave before stepping into that room. "You had to go through these two air locks to escape to the coast. They weren't taking any chances."

I follow her. "They who?"

"I've got some ideas," she replies, but offers no more as she leads me across the chamber to another four steps that ascend to a third pried-open door.

Another big truck passes overhead, followed by lighter traffic, but the vibrations no longer disturb me. I am troubled now by an even stronger premonition that ahead waits an unequaled abomination, an evil so pure, so perfectly vicious and thoroughly unwholesome that it belongs in a deeper level of Hell than any Dante ever imagined.

Past that third door, Jolie says, "From here on, there's power," and she presses a wall switch.

Warm light springs from tubes hidden in coves along both sides of a corridor that is as long as a football field, about twelve feet wide, maybe eight feet high. Every surface is pale yellow, shiny, and seems to be seamlessly plasticized.

The air is warmer here, and it has an astringent chemical smell that isn't unpleasant.

"When I first pried open that third set of doors," she says, "it was a lot warmer in here than this, and the smell was a lot stronger. I first thought the air might be bad for me, like toxic or something, but it doesn't irritate my throat or eyes, and if the stuff is gonna make me grow a second head, it hasn't happened yet."

Compared to the rooms preceding it, this space looks welcoming, but my presentiment of evil remains acute, and I'm glad that I have the pistol.

The girl says, "The next doors are powered-up and locked. Can't be pried open. All these barriers. So maybe there's a million bars of gold beyond it or the secret recipe for McDonald's special sauce. This hallway is as far as we can go."

About halfway to those distant doors, a figure lies on the hallway floor. At first it might be mistaken for a man, but then not.

As we approach the sprawled form, the girl says, "Whatever's beyond those last doors, if they *are* the last ones, there must not be anyone left over there. If anyone was over there, they wouldn't just leave the thing here so long. They'd take it away."

I can't tell for certain how tall the creature might have been in life or exactly what weight, because it appears to have mummified in the greater heat that she mentioned and in the chemical-laden air. As a guess, I would say it stood over seven feet and weighed short of three hundred pounds. But it is radically dehydrated, skin shrunken over its lanky body, over its long hands, and over the once-fearsome features of its huge head, skin as wrinkled as a gray linen suit worn hard and until threadbare and never once pressed.

What I *can* determine is that it is a primate, legs longer than its arms, more sophisticated than gorillas and other anthropoids, with a spinal curve like that of Homo sapiens, capable of standing fully erect. But there the similarity to a man ends, for this thing has long four-knuckled fingers, five per hand, and two three-knuckled thumbs per hand. Its toes are as long as its fingers, six per foot, with one thumblike toe in each half dozen.

"I call him Orc," the girl says.

"Why?"

"Well, I had to call him something, and *Bob* didn't seem right."

I don't know her yet, but I think I'm going to like her.

"Orc because he makes me think of the orcs in *The Lord of the Rings*."

Its skull, to which the flesh of the face has been shriveled and shrink-wrapped by the heat, is nearly the size and shape of a watermelon. The eyes have collapsed back into the desiccated brain, but judging by the sockets, they must have been the size of large lemons, set not horizontally like human eyes, but vertically. The remaining nose cartilage and a mass of shriveled tissue draped over it suggest a proboscis like that of an anteater, though three hooked lengths of hornlike structures, each two inches long, bristle from that portion of the face, unlike anything an anteater can boast. The lips have shrunk from the teeth, which are reminiscent of a wolf's oral weaponry. The mouth cracks uncommonly wide to allow the fullest use of that wickedly sharp and still-gleaming array of cutlery.

The presentiment of evil that has had its claws in me for most of the journey from the beach has not faded, but the reason for it is not this cadaver. Whatever alarms me is behind the closed doors at the end of this corridor, either living specimens related to this corpse or something worse.

One more thing strikes me as important. This carcass appears to be as dry as a mass of parchment, but no stains or time-hardened residue of decomposing tissues mars the floor under it. Where did the bodily fluids go, the dissolving and putrefying fats?

"I've been studying old Orc for a few months," the girl says.

"Studying him?"

"I can learn something from him. Something that'll help us. I'm sure I can."

"But . . . studying him here alone?"

No more than six feet from the body are a few folded, quilted blue moving blankets that Jolie has apparently provided for her comfort. She sits on one and folds her legs Indian-style.

"Orc doesn't scare me. Nothing much can scare me after five years of Dr. Hiskott."

"Who?"

The girl spells it for me. "The creep lives in what used to be our house. We're his animals to torment. Slaves, toys."

"The puppetmaster."

"Talking to you on the porch, Mom couldn't speak his name. He knows when it's used. But here I'm beyond the bastard's range. He can't hear me say how much I hate him, how much I want to kill him really hard."

I settle onto another folded moving blanket, facing her.

Jolie dresses to express the rebellion in which she dares not engage: dirty sneakers, jeans, a worn-denim jacket appliquéd with decorative copper rivets to suggest chain mail, and a black T-shirt on which a white skull grins.

In spite of that outfit and the settled anger that hardens her face, her tender beauty is greater than her mother has been able to convey. She is one of those girls who, though a tomboy, would always be chosen to play an angel in the church Christmas pageant and would be cast as the secular saint in any school play. Her beauty has no significant quality of nascent sexuality, but rather she is luminous and projects a goodness and an innocence that is a reflection of that profound grace we sometimes glimpse in nature and from which we take assurance that the world is a place of exquisite purpose.

"Dr. Hiskott. Where did he come from, Jolie?"

"He says Moonlight Bay. That's a couple miles up the coast. But we think he really came from Fort Wyvern."

"The army base?"

"Yeah. Just inland from Moonlight Bay—and from here. Humongous."

"How humongous?"

"Like 134,000 acres. A small city. Civilian workers, military guys, their families—forty thousand people used to live there. Not counting."

"Not counting what?"

"Things like Orc."

The lighting in the cove flutters, dims, goes out, and comes back on before I can bolt to my feet.

"Don't freak," the girl says sweetly. "It happens now and then."

"How many nows and how many thens?"

"It never stays dark more than a couple seconds. Besides, I've got a flashlight, you've got a gun."

As I am not one to unnecessarily frighten children and as I wish not to further frighten myself, I refrain from suggesting that what comes for us in the dark might find my pistol as unimpressive as her mini flashlight.

"Anyway," she says, "they closed Wyvern after the end of the Cold War, before I was born. People say there were secret projects at Wyvern, new weapons, experiments."

Looking at the mummified creature, I ask, "What experiments?"

"No one knows for sure. Weird stuff. Maybe messing around with genes, crap like that. Some say there's still something going on there, even though it's officially closed."

A bass electronic noise pulses along the hall, a *whummm-whummm-whummm* that seems to stir the marrow in my bones.

"That happens sometimes, too," the girl says. "I don't know what it is. Don't worry about it. Nothing ever happens after it."

I look toward the sealed doors she has been unable to open. "You think this connects with . . . someplace in Wyvern?"

"Well, I don't think it's a space-warp shortcut to Disney World. Anyway, Dr. Hiskott is sick when he checks into the motor court. He seems exhausted, confused, his hands shaking. My aunt Lois registers him. When he takes his driver's license from his wallet, he scatters a bunch of cards on the counter. Aunt Lois helps gather them up. She says one was a photo ID for Fort Wyvern. Before she married my uncle Greg, back when Wyvern was still open, she worked there."

"Why would he still carry a card years after the place closed?"

"Yeah, why?"

I don't have to be a mentalist to read, in her direct green gaze, that we both know the answer to my question.

"Hiskott stays in his cottage three days, won't let the maid change the linens or clean. And then he wasn't just Dr. Hiskott anymore. He was . . . something else, and he took control."

The electronic sound comes again, a longer series of notes than before: *Whummm-whummm-whummm-whummm-whummm.* . . .

Although shriveled, shrunken, mummified, and long dead, the bony fingers of Orc's left hand tap the floor, making a rattle like dancing dice, and from its gaping mouth comes an eager keening.

The lights flutter and go out.

PART TWO

Two-Part Harmony

Secret, and self-contained,
and solitary as an oyster.
                    —Charles Dickens, *A Christmas Carol*

Eight

DARKNESS HAS ITS CHARMS, AND EVEN IN OUR own hometowns, the world at night can be as enchanting as any foreign port with its exotic architectures. Between dusk and dawn, the commonplace is full of visual delights that only the moon, the stars, and richly textured shadows can provide.

But pitch-black gloom offers nothing except the fevered images of our imagination. And when we share absolute lightlessness with a grotesque mummy that makes a squalling-cat sound through its mouthful of buzz-saw teeth, the desire for light becomes so intense that we might set ourselves afire to provide it, if we had a match.

Fortunately, I have no match and am spared self-immolation, but Jolie Harmony has her mini flashlight, to which she resorts (if you want my considered opinion) much too slowly under the circumstances. When at last she does switch on that little torch, she aims it at me, or, more accurately, at my knees, as I am sitting on the floor of the corridor when the lights go out and the desiccated corpse begins to shriek, but then I erupt to my feet as abruptly as a spring-loaded novelty toothpick dispenser offering an afterdinner wooden probe. The beam is so narrow that it illumines only one of my knees, and instead of shifting it to her left, where the monstrous remains were last seen, the girl angles it upward, to my face, as if she's forgotten who she brought here and needs to confirm my identity.

Jolie is twelve and I'm almost twenty-two, so it is incumbent upon me to act like the adult in the room—or the corridor. I must not scream like a little girl, because the little girl herself isn't screaming. Before this adventure reaches an end, being human, I will no doubt have made a fool of myself in any number of ways; therefore, the longer I can delay behaving idiotically, the less humiliating it will be when I have to face her for our good-byes just before I ride off into the sunset with my faithful companion, Tonto. So with more aplomb than I expect, I blink into the light and in measured tones I say, "Show me the mummy."

The beam travels along my stiff arms to the pistol that I have in a two-hand grip, lowers from the pistol to the floor, and sweeps a few feet to the left, revealing that my blind aim is off-target. The creature, for which I have no biological classification, is still lying on its back, in the withered posture of a juiceless death. The only part of it that moves is its left hand, the bony fingers rattling against the floor as if in life it was a pianist and still longs to pound out some hot jazz on a keyboard.

My understanding thus far has been that this fallen beast is a dry husk surrounding a brittle skeleton that encloses the dust to which all creatures—those of us who are monsters and those of us who aren't—ultimately return. I *like* that understanding and can cope with it. This seeking hand is too much.

I stand over the thing, holding the pistol, pleased to see that my hands are shaking less than might be expected, certainly less than those of an octogenarian with familial tremors.

The cove lights along both sides of the corridor come on, and in that same moment, the mummy's caterwauling ceases. Its tapping hand falls still.

As Jolie switches off her mini flashlight and puts it on the floor beside her, I wonder aloud, "What the hell just happened?"

She's still sitting cross-legged on her folded moving blanket. She shrugs. "It never amounts to more than that."

"You said nothing ever happens after the *whummm-whummm-whummm* thing."

"I forgot about this."

"How could you forget such a thing?"

"It doesn't happen a whole lot. It's rare. The hand business is like a postmortem reflex or something."

"Totally dehydrated mummies don't have postmortem reflexes."

"Well, it's something," she says. "I've thought about cutting Orc open, you know, dissecting him, see what's in there."

"That's a bad idea."

"Orc is harmless. And I might learn something important."

"Yeah, you'll learn Orc isn't harmless. And what about the way it was screaming?"

"Wasn't screaming," the girl says. "Mouth didn't move. Chest didn't rise and fall. And if you think about it, that sound was electronic like the *whummm* but different, freakier. What seems to make sense is that something broadcast the sound, and Orc's dead vocal cords or its bones or something inside it is maybe like a receiver that just happened to pick up the transmission."

She sits there on her blanket, like little Miss Muffet on a tuffet, except that if a spider sits down beside her, she won't be scared away. She'll just crush it in her hand.

I lower my pistol, giving Orc the benefit of the doubt. "Good grief, kid, the first time the lights went out and you heard it, you were here alone?"

"Yeah."

"And you came *back*?"

"Like I told you, after years of Hiskott, I'm not afraid of much. I've seen lots that's terrible. I saw my cousin Maxy . . . murdered by Hiskott using my family to do the killing."

She has suffered so much, and that sorrows me. But she has been strong in the face of unthinkable adversity, and that inspires me.

"Please sit down, Mr. Potter."

"How do you know my name?"

"It's what you told Hiskott when he was controlling Uncle Donny. And he told us to stay away from you."

I almost reveal my true identity to her. Then I realize that if she leaves this subterranean refuge and returns to the Corner, within the puppetmaster's range, he might seize control of the girl, read her memory, and know my real name.

They say that voodoo priests, witches, and warlocks can't lay a spell upon you if they don't know your true name. That's probably superstitious hogwash. Anyway, this Hiskott guy isn't a voodoo priest or a witch or a warlock.

Nevertheless, I decide to keep my true name to myself for the time being.

Until the recent scare gave me my first white hairs, I

had been sitting on the floor, facing the girl, with the mummified monstrosity a few feet to my right. Now I reposition the blanket and sit with a clear view of both Jolie and Orc.

"You said those three days in his cottage, Hiskott was sick and then he changed, he wasn't just Hiskott anymore. What do you mean—that you don't think he had this power when he checked in, that it came to him somehow while he was staying there?"

Now Jolie, who was seven when life in the Corner changed, relies on family legend, which has been crafted and polished around dinner tables and firesides, in days of despondency and days of fragile but enduring hope, when they dared not discuss rebellion and, instead, told and retold one another the stories of their years of oppression, thereby transforming their suffering into a tale of endurance from which they could draw courage.

As that legend has it, Dr. Norris Hiskott arrives in a Mercedes S600, a far more high-end vehicle than what the average guest at their motor court drives. On first appearance, he seems to have been born for this day. Since dawn, a cold breeze has come off the sea, tinctured with an iodine scent from masses of decomposing seaweed that storm waves flung across near-shore rock formations two days earlier. The disturbing odor, the penetrating chill, and the curdled gray sky, lowering by the hour with a pending storm of predicted ferocity, have combined to raise in the Harmonys a mild, persistent disquiet. When registering Norris Hiskott in Cottage 9, Aunt Lois thinks it's curious that he's wearing Gucci loafers, expensive tailored slacks, a gold Rolex—and a hooded jersey tattered at the cuffs and stained as if he fished it out of a Dumpster. Although some people might feel the day is cold enough to justify gloves, the pair he's wearing are as peculiar as the jersey. These are gardening gloves, and he does not take them off. Likewise, he keeps the hood up throughout the registration process. Aunt Lois thinks perhaps some kid would wear a hoodie indoors, but not usually a man of about fifty and not one of this man's social position and sophistication. He seems furtive, as well, never making eye contact.

From what Jolie previously said, I hadn't inferred that the change in Hiskott that brought him this cruel power also altered him physically in some disastrous way. But this makes sense of his envy and of his too-beautiful-to-live decrees.

Holed up in Cottage 9, he refuses maid service, on the pretense that he is gravely ill with the flu, yet he seems to have a healthy appetite, for he orders a lot of take-out from the diner. Leaving his door unlocked, he asks that the food be left on the small table beside the armchair in the sitting area, and he leaves money for the charges plus tip. Hiskott remains in the bathroom while the delivery is made.

When he has been transformed by whatever virus or invading genetic material or other contamination he contracted in his work at Fort Wyvern, he moves quickly to claim this plot of ground as his perverse kingdom. His sphere of influence reaches in most places to the boundaries of the Corner, falls short here and there, extends farther in a few areas. Because of the awful changes in his appearance, he will most likely never be able to venture into the world beyond this property.

All brain activity is electrical, and Hiskott is able to calve off an aspect of his personality: Think of it as a memory stick of everything he knows and is, but without the stick, contained instead in a coherent electric field. With certain limitations of distance, he is able to transmit this other essentially invisible self, this phantom Hiskott, through telephone land lines or by means of other systems, such as power lines and water pipes and television cables, or a combination thereof. Like a snake, this Hiskott data bundle is able to coil in a TV, a lamp, an appliance; and when a potential host ventures near enough, it can leap to him and take possession, while the real Hiskott remains in seclusion elsewhere.

Instantaneously, the data bundle, acting rather like a computer virus, does not merely seize control of whomever it invades but also downloads into the host's brain a program making that person's lifetime of memories available to Hiskott. Task complete, the phantom Hiskott returns to the real Hiskott; thereafter, within Harmony Corner, he enjoys a permanent communications link to the person whom he has violated, as well as a control function that, at his whim, allows him to remotely operate that person's body as if it were his own.

All of this is at once fully understood by each person over whom Hiskott claims sovereignty. And each is acutely aware that his puppetmaster can kill him in an endless variety of ways, not least of all by shutting down the autonomic nervous system that controls the automatic functions of organs, blood vessels, and glands—which will bring instant death.

If one of them bolts beyond the Corner and doesn't return, retaliation will be directed upon those family members whom the escapee loves most. Their deaths will be cruel and slow and painful in the extreme, but also they will be subjected to such imaginative abominations as to fill them with humiliation, with such shame that their contempt for themselves will exceed their fear of death. The one who got away will carry a weight of guilt that eventually will make life intolerable.

Escaping with the intent to return with the police or cavalry of some other kind will be futile. The escapee will probably soon find himself needing to escape again, this time from a psychiatric ward, to which his tale of mind control has gotten him committed as surely as if he angrily claims to be Godzilla and threatens to destroy Los Angeles. In the unlikely event that authorities could be convinced of an extraordinary threat to such an apparently peaceful place as Harmony Corner, when they arrive on scene, Hiskott will take them one by one. Because those outsiders can never be allowed to return to their offices with knowledge of Norris Hiskott or with any suspicion whatsoever, he won't possess them in the same manner as he does the Harmonys, but he will instead slip deep into their minds as unobtrusively as a cold virus invading the lungs on an inhalation. He will edit and massage their thoughts without their awareness, and he will send them away with memories that he crafts for them.

Until Jolie tells me this, I have not understood how complete is the stranglehold that Hiskott has on them. That the members of the Harmony family have persevered, held fast to their sanity, and remained hopeful is a feat almost beyond my comprehension.

Orc lies quiet.

Boo materializes and examines the mummified remains with great curiosity.

The girl doesn't see the dog. She and I sit in contemplative silence.

Finally I ask, "Hiskott, whoever he was and whatever he now is—what does he want?"

"Control. Obedience."

"But why?"

"Because of the way he now looks, he can't be seen in public, he's gross. He lives through us."

For a moment, another question more intrigues me: "What does he look like?"

"When he moved from Cottage 9 to the house he took from us, he did it at night. We weren't allowed to see."

"But in five years, taking food to him, cleaning his house—surely someone's gotten a glimpse of him."

She nods and seems to need a moment to gather herself before approaching this subject. "Only Uncle Greg and Aunt Lois. And Hiskott's made it impossible for them to share what they've seen. Implanted a prohibition in their minds."

"Prohibition?"

She is a serious girl but still a child, lively in the way of children and eager for wonder and delight, serious but not to the exclusion of the possibility of joy, as an oppressed adult might be. But now a new solemnity overcomes her, and she looks so grave that I can see the worn and weary woman that she might become as more years of enslavement grind her down, and I am almost unable to look at her because it might fall to me, and me alone, to either help or fail her.

Eyes downcast and hands plucking nervously at her

denim jacket, with a tic tweaking the corner of her left eye, she says, "Greg and Lois tried. They tried to tell us. About his appearance. Twice they really tried. But each time they bit their tongues. They bite hard. Tongues, lips. Chew their lips until they bleed. The only words they can get out are obscenities. Blasphemies. Awful words they wouldn't say unless forced to. They spit out the blood, the words, and for days their mouths are too sore to eat. They don't dare try to tell us a third time. We don't want them to try. We don't need to know. It doesn't matter. Knowing won't change things."

We need another silence.

Boo wanders away from Orc and along the hallway toward the doors that Jolie could not pry open.

In time I return to our previous subject. "Control. Obedience. But why?"

"Like I said. Because of how he looks, he has to live through us, me and my folks. He can eat. He can drink. But there is so much he can't do. He's like an oyster or something and that house on the hill is his shell. He tells us we're his sensorium."

Jolie raises her head, and her eyes are the green of lotus leaves. She stops plucking at her denim jacket. Like doves floating to a roost, her hands settle on her knees. The tic is gone from the corner of her left eye. Speaking of her aunt's and uncle's suffering distresses and agitates her. I think this subject distresses and agitates her, too, and perhaps even to a greater degree. But to speak of it at all, she needs to impose upon herself, with a kind of yogic application of willpower, a serenity that allows her to comment from the clear upper air that lies above all storm and shadow.

She says, "You know what a sensorium is?"

"No."

"Like the sensory apparatus of the body. All the sensory organs, nerves. Through me—through us—he's able to have the world that he can't be seen in anymore. Not just the sights and sounds and tastes but all of that from lots of different perspectives, from all of our perspectives instead of just one. And what he's unable to experience there in his shell, in his gross body that no eye would want to look upon or hand would want to touch, he can feel by living in us, by feeling what we feel, sharing our sensations, requiring us to provide whatever experience he wants most at any moment. There's no privacy in the Corner. There's no place in your heart where you can be alone to feel sorry for yourself, to heal from the latest thing he did to you. He crawls in there with you. He drinks your sorrow and mocks your hope of healing."

I am badly shaken.

Chronologically she is twelve, but emotionally she is older, and intellectually older still.

Compared to her deep strength, I am weak. I am a fumbling fry cook trying to do the best he can with his strange sixth sense, but she is Joan of Arc, fighting against impossible odds, not for her country but for her soul—while Hiskott, in the reach of his power and considering his cruelty, is a more formidable enemy than even the army of England. Jolie, who began this war with the inadequate arms and defenses of a seven-year-old child, has triumphed merely by enduring, has raised the siege of Orléans every day for five long years, and it seems to me that I am in the presence of one who might be a saint in the making.

Now I fully understand why she has no fear of Orc. Or perhaps of anything.

At the end of the hallway, head cocked and curious, Boo stands before the sealed pair of stainless-steel doors.

Jolie says, "This time, with you here, if Hiskott tries to possess me while I'm beyond his reach, and he can't find me . . . well, then he'll kill me as soon as I reappear."

"So you'll stay here until I can take him down."

"I can't stay here forever and ever," she says.

"And I don't have forever. Today. It's got to be done today—and sooner than later."

She has restrained her curiosity until now. "Why can't he get into your mind and possess you?"

"I don't know, Jolie. But I always have been hard-headed."

"I don't believe that."

"Maybe I just don't have much of a mind for him to get his tentacles around."

"Or that. He says he can't access the woman with you, either."

"That's good to know."

"Who is she?"

Getting to my feet, I say, "Now *that* is the million-dollar question."

"You don't know who she is?"

"I just met her yesterday. I know her first name. That's a start. In a year or two, I'll know her last name, if she has a last name, which she says she doesn't."

Rising to her feet, Jolie says, "Are you always a little silly?"

"I'm usually a *lot* silly."

"It'll get you killed in the Corner."

"Maybe not. So far, being at least a little silly has kept me alive."

"He'll have them all searching for you, anyone who doesn't have to be up at the diner or the service station. You can't go anywhere in the Corner without being seen."

"Well, I'm just an ordinary, everyday, nothing-special fry cook. People tend to look right through guys like me."

She stares at me solemnly for a beat, but then she proves to be still capable of a small smile.

I would give just about anything to hear Jolie laugh one day. I don't think she's laughed in a long time.

At the end of the hallway, my ghost dog walks through the steel doors.

Nine

BEFORE I LEAVE THE FEARLESS GIRL WITH ORC
the inhuman mummy in the subterranean passageway
between the possessed land of Harmony and the unknown
government-sponsored atrocities of Wyvern (which makes
this already as unusual a sentence as any I've ever written
in these memoirs), she tells me one more important thing
that I should know before I try to beard the lion in his
den.

And speaking of peculiar language, why do we say *beard*
the lion instead of *confront* the lion? The image it brings
to mind is of me crawling recklessly into a cave to use
spirit gum to attach a fake beard to a sleeping feline of
daunting size. Because no lion is ever going to be induced
to play Abraham Lincoln in a stage play, there would seem

to be no reason to glue a beard on a lion other than to poke fun at it and laugh at its humiliation as the other lions mock it mercilessly. I'm sure that Ozzie Boone knows the origin of that expression, and no doubt our finest universities are crawling with intellectuals who have spent their entire academic careers writing papers about bearding lions—not to mention thick, learned volumes about the derivation of such sayings as *belling the cat* and *spanking the monkey*—but from time to time I am saddened to think that I will almost certainly not live long enough or have sufficient leisure to research such peculiarities of language myself, which I might enjoy doing.

Anyway, the one additional thing of importance that Jolie has to tell me before I leave her is this: Although Hiskott is secretive and self-contained, he doesn't live alone in the big house on the hill. Over the years, he has read the memories—and sometimes taken temporary control—of guests who stay in the motor-court cottages, and on three occasions, he has asserted permanent dominion over them and has taken them into his house, whereafter they are never seen again. In every case, these seem to be individuals who are pretty much loners, without families who might miss them. After stripping the plates off those people's cars, Donny parks them in the deep shade of a grove of oaks, halfway down the hills between the motor court and the family's houses, where they are cannibalized for parts as the service station needs them and are allowed otherwise to fall into ruin. Food and anything else Hiskott demands is brought to him by the family, but no one has cleaned for him in over three years; therefore none of the Harmonys has seen the inside of the house since the first of those three luckless souls walked zombie-like through the front door.

"So it seems they do the cleaning," Jolie says. "But we're pretty sure they aren't just used like we are. He's got some other purpose for them, which is why he never lets us see them."

"Maybe he uses them as his Praetorian Guard, his ultimate protectors, in case one of your family should ever slip the leash and try to kill him."

"Like bodyguards." Clearly she long ago came to this conclusion and has given it considerable thought without finding it a fully satisfactory explanation. "But why wouldn't he be just as worried that one of *them* might slip the leash?"

So many things in my continuing education are learned by going where I have to go and doing what I have to do. Therefore, my only answer is: "I guess I'll find out."

Jolie surprises me by throwing her arms around me and pressing one ear against my chest, as though listening to my heart to judge the strength, steadiness, and truth of it. She is more than a foot shorter than I am, so slight for such a strong girl.

I return the hug, suddenly certain that I will fail her, though since childhood I have expected myself to fail much more often than I actually do.

"I've waited five years for you," she says. "I knew you'd come one day. I always knew."

Perhaps to her I'm a knight in shining armor who cannot fail to win the day. I know that I am less capable and less noble than the knights of folklore and fairy tales. My only armor is my belief that life has meaning and that, when my last sun has set and my last moon has risen, when the dawn comes that marks the moment when I am born with the dead, there will be mercy. If thinking me a knight nourishes her hope, however, I might count myself a success for having done this if nothing more.

When we step back from each other, she has no tears to wipe away, because she is beyond easy sentimentality and too tough to cry for herself. Her eyes are lotus-leaf green, but she is no lotus-eater; she has survived not by forgetting but by remembering. I see in her a diligent accountant who records the puppetmaster's every offense in a mental ledger. When the day comes to settle accounts, she will know what his payment must be. Although she is young and small, she will do whatever she can to help her family wring from him the full and terrible balance that he owes.

"I'll do my best to get him," I promise. "But my best might not be good enough."

"Whatever," she says. "You won't just run and save yourself. I *know* you won't. You run toward things, not away from them. I don't know who you are, except you're not Harry Potter. There's something about you, I don't know what it is, but it's something, and it's good."

Only a worse fool than I would reply to that, for any response would diminish either her or me, or both of us. Such genuine trust, so sweetly expressed, bears witness to an innocence in the human heart that endures even in this broken world and that longs to ring the bell backward and undo the days of history until all such trust would be justified in a world started anew and as it always should have been.

"Jolie, I'll need a flashlight to find my way out. But I don't want to leave you here without one, in case these lights go off again and stay off."

"I've got two." She fishes the second mini flashlight from a pocket of her denim jacket and presents it to me.

"The big pipe that we followed up through the hills and out of the Corner—do other tributary drains feed it?"

"Yeah. Five. When you're going back—three to your left, two on your right. You can't walk upright in any of them. You have to stoop. Sometimes you have to crawl."

"Tell me where they go."

"Nowhere. At the end of each, it's been sealed off. I don't know why or when. But storm water hasn't been flowing through those drains in a long time, maybe ever since the people at Fort Wyvern connected their escape hatch to the system—if it is an escape hatch."

"So I can't go anywhere except back to the beach."

"No. But I don't think they'll be waiting there for you. See . . . well, there's something else. But if I tell you, I don't want it to be another weight on your mind. You've got enough to worry about."

"Tell me anyway. I love to worry. I'm aces at it."

She hesitates. From a hip pocket of her jeans, she extracts a slim wallet, flips it open, and shows me a photograph of a handsome boy of about eight.

"Is that Maxy?"

"Yeah. Hiskott said Maxy had to die 'cause he was too beautiful. He really was a cute little boy. So we're supposed to think it was envy because Hiskott has changed into something super-ugly. But I don't think that's why he killed Maxy."

Even as tough as she has become, Jolie is silenced by grief. A tremor of the mouth tests her composure, but she presses her lips together. She folds the lost boy away and returns him to her pocket.

"Lately," she continues, "he's been taunting all of us, using my family to tell me I'm beautiful, more beautiful than Maxy. He's trying to terrify me and torment all the others with the thought that he'll use them to beat me and rip me apart the way he used them to kill Maxy. But it's a lie."

"What's a lie?"

"I'm not beautiful."

"But Jolie . . . you really are."

She shakes her head. "I don't see it. I don't believe it. I know it's a lie. I can't be beautiful. Not after what I did."

"What do you mean?"

With one foot, she pushes a folded moving blanket close to Orc. She kneels on it, staring down into the creature's shriveled face.

When she speaks, her voice is controlled, allowing no sharp emotions that might be suitable to her words, colored only by a quiet melancholy. "It starts, and it's horrible. I'm screaming at them to stop, pleading. One after another of them going at Maxy—my family, his family. And they were trying to restrain each other. They were trying. But Hiskott moves so fast, from this one to that one, you never know where he's going next. Such violent kicking, punching, gouging. Maxy's blood . . . on everyone. I can't stop them, Maxy's almost dead, and I've got to run away, I can't bear to see the end of it."

With no evident distaste, with a deliberate tenderness, Jolie lifts the hand with which the briefly animated, mummified cadaver had tapped the floor.

Examining the wickedly long fingers, she says, "I start to run but then I'm standing over Maxy, and I don't know where I got the knife that's in my hand. Big knife. He's not quite dead. Bewildered, half conscious. He's just eight. I'm nine. He recognizes me. His eyes clear for a moment. I stab him once and then again. And again. And that's the end of him."

Her silence has such substance that for a moment I'm not able to force words into it. But then: "It wasn't you, Jolie."

"In a way, it was."

"No, it wasn't."

"In a way," she insists.

"He was controlling you."

In that awful voice of tightly tethered sorrow, in words too mature for her age, she says, "But I saw it. Lived it. I felt flesh and bone resist the knife. I saw him seeing me when the life went out of his eyes."

My sense is that if I drop to my knees beside her and try to comfort her, she will not allow herself to be hugged as before. She will thrash away from me, and the bond between us will be damaged. This is her grief, to which she clings in honor of her murdered cousin, and this is her guilt that, although unearned, is perhaps proof to her that in spite of what she was made to do, she is still human. I know a great deal about grief and guilt, but while this is like unto my grief and guilt, it is *not* mine, and I have no right to tell her what she should feel.

Lowering the monster's hand to the floor, she returns again to the study of its face, in particular the large sockets at the bottoms of which lie the mottled and furred tissue that is what remains of its eyes, like the once flourishing but now fossilized mold at the bottom of a long-dry well. Again the cove lighting flutters, does not go out this time, but summons throbs of shadow from those bony orbits, so that it seems a pair of eyes repeatedly roll left to right and back again, entirely black eyes like those of Death might be when he shows up on a doorstep with an eviction notice.

"I'm not beautiful. That's not the reason he's getting ready to kill me. During the past few months, there are times when he seeks me and can't find me because I'm here. And later, when he takes me and reads me, in my memories it seems I was always somewhere ordinary where he should have found me. For a while he thought the fault was in him, but he now suspects I've learned how to hide a thing or two that I don't want him to know."

The power to shut out the puppeteer from even a small part of her memory should be a hopeful development, but she seems to take no hope from it.

"And is he right? Have you learned to hide a thing or two?"

"They say you should study languages when you're just

a kid, because you get them a lot faster than when you're grown up. I think it's that way with figuring how to fake out Hiskott. I can't hide much, but a little more month by month, including this place, where I go to escape him. I don't believe any of the adults have been able to do that, but I think Maxy might have been about where I am now when he was killed. Maybe Hiskott suspected Maxy. Maybe he was afraid Maxy might learn to resist being taken, so he murdered him."

"You think you could learn to keep him out, deny him control?"

"No. Not for years if ever. And he won't let me live that long. But there's another thing I did."

She lightly taps a forefinger against the points of Orc's lower teeth, moving left to right along the cadaver's sharkish grin.

If Orc's hand can abruptly drum fingers against the floor, its jaws, which seem to be locked open by withered tendons and shrunken muscles, might snap shut on her tender fingertips.

I consider warning her. But she surely has thought of the same danger, and she will ignore me. Something about this moment suggests that it is neither Orc's existence nor its origins that intrigues Jolie, nor any particular feature of its demonic face. Instead, brow furrowed, testing the cutting edges of her teeth with her tongue as she assesses

Orc's array of daggers with her finger, she seems to be contemplating a question that worries her.

And then she puts her concern into words: "Does a monster know it's a monster?"

Her question appears simple, and some might find it ridiculous because, as modern thinkers know, psychology and theories of social injustice can explain the motives of all who ever commit an evil act, revealing them to be in fact victims themselves; therefore such things as monsters do not exist—no Minotaurs, no werewolves, no orcs, and likewise no Hitlers, no Mao Tse-tungs. But I can guess why she is asking the question, and in this context it is a complex inquiry of profound importance to her.

Jolie deserves a thoughtful and nuanced answer, although in our current circumstances, a textured reply will only encourage in her further self-doubt. We don't have time for such uncertainty because it reliably breeds indecision, and indecision is one of the mothers of failure.

"Yes," I assure her. "A monster knows it's a monster."

"Always and everywhere?"

"Yes. A monster not only knows that it's a monster, but it also *enjoys* being a monster."

She meets my eyes. "How do you know?"

Indicating Orc, I say, "This isn't my first monster. I've had experience with all kinds of them. Mostly the human kind. And the human kind *especially* revel in their evil."

Returning her attention to the teeth, the girl seems to consider what I have said. To my relief, she stops risking a bite and touches instead the creature's large, bulbous brow, where the crinkled skin sheds a few flakes under her forefinger.

"Anyway," she says, wiping her finger on her jeans, "there's another thing I did, besides keeping from him the place I go when he can't find me. I imagined this secret cave, hidden by brush, high in the hills, as far from the culvert on the beach as you can get and still be in the Corner. And yesterday, when he took me for a while, I let him see the cave in my memory, as if it were real, but not where it's supposed to be. So now that he's ready to kill me, maybe he'll waste time using some of the family to search for the cave."

"How can you be sure he's ready . . . for that?"

"Too much is slipping out of his control. You know about him, so he's got to kill you. Then he'll kill the lady with you because he can't control her. He was going to kill me in a day or two, before you showed up, so he'll just go ahead and do it as soon as he's finished with you two."

Annamaria seems to have uncanny knowledge superior to mine. She says she's safe in the Corner. Maybe. Maybe not. I wish I could be in two places at once.

"I'll get him first."

"I think you might. But if you don't . . . the three of us

will be buried in the meadow beside Maxy, with no coffins and no headstones."

She gets to her feet once more and stands with her hands on her hips. In her skull T-shirt and rivet-decorated jacket, she looks both defiant and vulnerable.

"If Hiskott gets you first," she says, "what I need is a little extra time while he's looking for the cave that doesn't exist, just a little extra time to get ready to be killed. I don't want to beg or scream. I don't want to cry if I can help it. When he uses my family to kill me, I want to be able to keep telling them how much I love them, that I don't blame them, that I'll pray for them."

Ten

THIS IS NOT ONE OF THE EASIEST THINGS I HAVE ever done: leaving Jolie alone with the mummified remains in the yellow yet nonetheless dreary corridor, which could as likely be the path to Hell or, worse, one of those airport passageways that leads inevitably to a coven of transportation-agency employees eager to strip-search Grandma, anal-probe a nun, and invite one and all to submit to a body scan that will trigger either bone cancer or the growth of a third eye in an inconvenient place. My ghost dog isn't even here to watch over her.

On the other hand, she has been alone in this hallway on many previous occasions. She is most likely safer here than anywhere in the Corner. Besides, although she *is* a girl and a child, she has as much hair on her chest, figuratively speaking, as I do.

With the mini flashlight in one hand and the pistol in the other, I retrace the route along which she led me: through pried-open doors, across two spacious air locks or decontamination chambers. In the stainless-steel walls, holes like the muzzles of rifles take aim at me.

When I arrive at the concrete culvert that previously we passed through in absolute darkness, I pause to sweep the narrow beam over the walls. I am reminded of a maze of such drains about which I wrote in the second volume of these memoirs; in that place I was almost killed more than once. Of course, I can't allow myself to be wary of one place merely because it reminds me of another place where I almost died, because just about *every* place reminds me of another place where I almost died, whether it's a police station or a church, or a monastery, or a casino, or an ice-cream shop. I've never almost died in a laundromat or a McDonald's, or a sushi bar, but then I'm not yet quite twenty-two, and with luck, I'll have a lot more years in which to almost die in all kinds of venues.

I start along the inclined drain, recalling the original version of *Invaders from Mars*, 1953, in which evil scheming Martians secretly establish a subterranean fortress under a quiet American town, and actors wearing costumes with visible zippers up the back pretend to be otherworldly monsters, lumbering through tunnels on one nefarious mission or another. In spite of the zippers, it's an eerie flick, a minor science-fiction classic, but there's nothing in it as scary as half the people on any Sunday-morning episode of *Meet the Press*.

Before I've gone far, I come to the first tributary drain on the right, which is as Jolie described it: about five feet in diameter, navigable only in a stoop. Because the girl previously explored this branch of the drains and knows that the end is sealed, I have no intention of taking a side trip.

As I'm passing the opening, however, a noise halts me. Issuing from a distance, echoing along that smaller tunnel, arises a low rumbling-grinding sound as though some heavy metal object is moving across concrete. The flashlight beam doesn't reach far, and just as I wonder if I'm hearing an immense iron ball rolling toward me, set loose by a malevolent alien with a zipper up its back, the sound stops.

At once a draft springs up, smelling faintly of aged concrete. This is not the stale air of sluggish circulation through lightless realms. It's fresh and clean, whispering against my face, ever so slightly stirring my hair, as pleasantly cool as morning air should be on a January day along the central California coast.

If the upper end of this drain was previously sealed, it

is evidently not sealed now. Who opened it and why are of immediate importance, because the timing is unlikely to be coincidental.

No further noise ensues, no slightest sound of anyone descending.

Although no one is likely to have seen Jolie and me fleeing to the beach in the moonless dark, though the girl has misdirected Hiskott—and therefore everyone else—to the nonexistent cave, I am not enthusiastic about returning to the shore. Any other exit from this system might offer advantages over the vine-draped terminus of the main culvert.

With the frequently but not always reliable intuition of a clairvoyant fry cook, I sense that this alternate route might be safe and that whoever unsealed this side drain might possibly be my friend or at least might prefer that Norris Hiskott die rather than that I die, or might rather see both of us dead instead of *just* me.

I decide to act without delay on this unnervingly qualified perception. After all, the worst that can happen is that I will be killed.

Proceeding in a stoop, darkness ahead and behind, gripping the pistol and the flashlight, almost dragging my knuckles on the floor, I feel like a troll except that of course I don't eat children, more like Gollum than a troll, Gollum leading Frodo the Hobbit into the lair of the giant, spiderlike Shelob, except that I'm more like Frodo than Gollum, being led rather than leading, which means I'm the one that will get stung, restrained by spun silken threads as tough as wire, and put aside so that later, at my captor's leisure, I can be eaten alive.

Somewhat to my surprise, there is no Shelob, and after it seems that I've gone nearly all the way to Mordor, my calves aching from the strain of walking in this gorilla posture, I arrive at the end of the tunnel. An iron ladder leads up to an open manhole through which falls the first pink light of morning.

When I lever myself out of the drain, I'm standing in a four-foot-wide concrete swale. Behind me, to the east, a long slope leads up to guardrails and the coast highway. In front of me is the county road that leads to Harmony Corner, which lies perhaps two hundred yards to my left. As night spills away to the western horizon and the flamingo dawn flocks more of the sky, I can see the quaint service station, the diner where several vehicles are parked as the breakfast rush begins, but not the cottages in their haven of trees.

If one of the Harmonys happens to see me, I'm at such a distance that he won't know who I am.

The hum of a motor draws my attention to the open manhole, where a series of stainless-steel wedges suddenly iris inward from its rim and lock together to form what must be a watertight seal. I'd like to believe that somewhere I have a friend. But instead I am troubled by the feeling that I'm being manipulated rather than assisted.

Every member of the Harmony family is a prisoner but also a weapon that can be used against me by Hiskott. I'm one. They're many. During the morning shift, perhaps a third of them have to work the family business, but the others are available to search for me and to protect Hiskott, which they have no choice but to do; especially in a crisis like this, if they dare to resist, he will use them to slaughter a few of their own.

I don't want to hurt any of them. Under current circumstances, I can't slip past so many and make my way to the house in which Norris Hiskott resides. Therefore, it's necessary to change the circumstances.

To the north lies the intersection between the county road and the exit ramp from the coast highway. As I walk toward it, I pocket the mini flashlight and tuck the pistol under my belt, against my abdomen, between my T-shirt and sweatshirt.

A hundred yards short of the intersection, I stop, drop to one knee, and wait on the shoulder of the roadway.

Within a minute, a Ford Explorer appears at the head of the exit ramp.

I pick up a small stone and pretend to be examining it as if it fascinates me. Maybe it's a nugget of gold or maybe nature has weathered into it a miraculously detailed portrait of Jesus.

The Explorer slows at the stop sign, glides through the intersection without making a full stop, turns left, and accelerates past me.

A couple of minutes later, when an eighteen-wheeler looms at the top of the ramp, I drop the stone and get to my feet.

What I'm about to do is bad. It's not as terrible as embezzling a billion dollars from the investment firm you run. It's not as bad as being a public servant who gets rich over a lifetime of taking bribes. But it's a lot worse than tearing the DO NOT REMOVE UNDER PENALTY OF LAW tag from the cushions of your new sofa. It's bad. Bad. I don't endorse my own actions. If my guardian angel is watching, he is no doubt appalled. If any young people read this memoir someday, I hope they are not inspired by my offense to commit similar offenses of their own. The same applies to elderly readers. We don't need a bunch of badly behaved retirees any more than we need young hoodlums. I can explain why I have to do what I'm about to do, but I'm acutely aware that an explanation is not a righteous justi-fication. What's bad is bad even if necessary. This is bad. I'm sorry. Okay, here we go.

Eleven

RIGHT THERE, RIGHT THEN, WHEN HE LEAVES me with orc to try to get Hiskott, I think I love him. I never thought I could. Love some guy, I mean. Or maybe what I mean is that I never thought I *should*. Not after what happened these past five years. Not after the awful thing that happened to Maxy. My expectation, if you want to know, has been that I'll go away and be a nun. I mean, if something were to happen to Hiskott and we were free again. A nun or a missionary in the worst slum in the world, where the cockroaches are as big as dachshunds and people are covered in festering sores and desperately need help. I know what it's like to desperately need help, and what I think is it would feel really good to be on the other side, to be able to give help to people who need it, desperately or otherwise. If you're going to be a nun or a missionary or even one of those doctors who work for nothing in countries that are so poor the people have no money, so they trade with one another using bricks of dry animal dung they can burn to heat their hovels and a few diseased chickens and maybe some edible tubers that they dig out of the floor of a snake-infested jungle . . . Well, what I mean is, if you're going to be any of those things, there's no time in your life for dating or romance or marriage, or anything. So what would be the point of loving a guy? Anyway, nuns aren't allowed to marry.

I think I love him just the same. It sure feels like love or what I think love should feel like. You'd probably say it happened too fast to be love, though they do say there's such a thing as love at first sight, so that's my answer to the too-fast criticism. Well, I do have to admit it's not the way he looks that knocked me flat. I think we could all agree Harry's no Justin Bieber. Of course he's not really Harry Potter, but it's what I have, so that's got to be his name for a while. Harry is adorable enough, he's cute, but lots of guys are cute, I guess, you see *herds* of them on TV. Why I love him is, I don't know, because he seems very brave and kind and sweet. All that stuff but something else, too. I don't know *what* something else, but he's different somehow, and what I'm trying to say is it's a good kind of difference, whatever it is.

There go the lights again, fluttering, and that *whummm-whummm* sound. Old Orc doesn't react this time. Orc doesn't always do his thing when the sound comes. Mostly, he just lies there being dead. I don't know why I like sitting with Orc. I've always felt safe with him. Maybe it's because he's dead and all, but I don't think that's the whole reason. He's so big and ugly you'd think nothing could ever kill him, but something sure enough did. So if something can kill old Orc, something can kill anything, even Dr. Norris Hiskott, so maybe that's why I really like sitting with Orc. I'm not a child—or at least I'm not a *naive* child who thinks whatever killed Orc will come along and offer to kill Hiskott for me. Nothing could ever be that easy. Hiskott says dying is easy and we should never forget how easy it is. But dying is never easy, and what he means is that *killing* is easy, at least for him.

The thing about me loving Harry is I'm twelve and he's maybe thirty or thirty-five, whatever, so he'll have to wait like six years for me to grow up. I mean if he kills Hiskott and sets us free, he'll have to wait. He'll never do that. As kind and sweet and brave as he is, he probably has a girl already and a hundred others chasing after him. So what I'll have to do is I'll have to always love him from afar. Unrequited love. That's what they generally call it. I'll love him forever in a deeply, deeply sad kind of way, which maybe you think sounds pretty depressing, but it isn't.

Being obsessed about a deeply sad unrequited love can take your mind off worse things, of which there are *thousands*, and sometimes it's better to dwell endlessly on what you can't have (which is Harry) than on what might happen to you at any moment in Harmony Corner (which is anything).

The *whummm-whummm* has stopped and the lights haven't gone out this time, and Orc just lies there, and Harry hasn't been gone long, though it feels like a decade since I last saw him. When you're in love, I guess time gets all distorted. And not only when you're in love. When my aunt Lois tried to kill herself and all, she said it was because she felt like she'd been trapped in the Corner for a hundred years, but that was two years ago, so it wasn't a hundred, it was only three. Uncle Greg caught her before she did it, and the way he cried and cried, Aunt Lois realized what she almost did was pretty selfish, and she's never tried it again. Mom says what keeps *her* from trying what Aunt Lois tried is me, the way I handle all this for a girl so young. Mom's been saying that same thing for years, which is why I know I have to be tough and handle it without going nuts or bawling my eyes out. The thing is, if you get what I mean, by staying hopeful and not moping around in a black depression, I'm keeping both of us alive until something happens. And something will, something good, and maybe that's Harry, who's now been gone for like twenty years.

I get up from the floor, figuring I should pace the corridor back and forth until I wear the edge off my nerves or just collapse unconscious from exhaustion, so I don't have to worry about Harry, and just then something pretty interesting happens. The fourth door, the one I was never able to pry open, now opens with a *whoosh*. On the other side there's just darkness, which at first seems a little threatening, as you might imagine. I'm like, should I run or not, but there's nowhere to run except back to the Corner, where Hiskott can find me as easy as a bird can find a worm, not that I mean he's a bird and I'm a worm. *He's* the worm.

Anyway, nothing comes out of the darkness over there, and after a minute or so, I don't feel so threatened anymore. Walking toward the open doors, I say hello, but no one answers me. So I say that my name is Jolie Ann Harmony, as if maybe someone's in the darkness but won't speak to a stranger, which is pretty dumb when you think about it. But after five years as a prisoner of Hiskott, nobody should expect my social skills to be super-great or anything.

I'm standing right on the threshold, and still I can't see ten inches into the room beyond, it's so black in there. I have my little flashlight, so I can explore if I want, and let's face it, there's nothing else to do here except go crazy, which I can't do on account of my mom. Anyway, crazy isn't me.

I return to Orc to fetch a moving blanket, which I roll tight. At the doorway again, I lay the blanket roll across the threshold so that the doors can't close behind me and I can get back from wherever I'm going.

Just then, far out there in the dark, a yellow light comes on. I wait, but it isn't getting closer, it's a fixed lamp somewhere, and maybe someone turned it on to let me know where I need to go and all, because they know I don't have a clue, which I don't mean as a put-down of myself, it's just the truth in this particular case.

When I cross the threshold, the floor in this new place is like hard rubber, you almost bounce along it. When I say my name again just to see if maybe we can't start some conversation after all, my voice sounds as though I've got a flannel sack over my head and am talking from the bottom of a dry stone well, though I don't know why I'd ever be in such a situation unless some maniac serial killer stashed me down there for some unspeakable reason.

Also when I talk, the walls throb with blue light, so that I can see the room is maybe forty feet on a side. Those throbbing blue walls are covered with hundreds of cones sort of like what I saw once in a TV series where this guy was a talk-show host working in a sound booth in a radio station or somewhere. It's like the big cones are soaking up my voice but at the same time turning the sound of it into blue light, which didn't happen in the TV show. The faster and more I talk, the brighter the light becomes, sort of pulsing in time with my words.

If you want my opinion, it's a weird room, but it doesn't feel like a dangerous place. It's even kind of peaceful, though it does make you feel half deaf and makes your skin look blue like the freaky people on the planet in that movie *Avatar*. I mean, it's not the kind of room where you think maybe you'll find dead naked people hanging on chains from the ceiling. Anyway, there's plenty of blue light as long as I keep talking, so I start reciting a couple of Shel Silverstein poems I've memorized, and I verse myself all the way across the room to a big round opening you could drive a Mack truck through if you knew how to drive, which I don't. I can see through it to the yellow light that first drew me in here, if you remember, and it's still as far away as it ever was, as if it must be moving from me as fast as I head toward it.

When I try to go through this big round door, it turns out to be more of a window but not glass. It's cold and clear and kind of gummy, and when I try to step back from it, I can't. I'm not stuck in the stuff exactly, but it holds me, and then it seems to fold around me, which you can imagine sort of freaks me out, as if the stuff is going to seal me up in a clear cocoon and suffocate me. But then it turns out to be a door after all, and after it folds around me, the stuff unfolds, and I'm on the other side. I don't know, that doesn't quite explain how it feels. Maybe it's more like the clear stuff that fills the doorway is some giant amoeba that sucks you in from one room and spits you out into the next, except it isn't that, either.

Anyway, in the next room are six dead people all in those bulky white hazmat suits like you see on TV news when there's been a toxic-chemical spill or clouds of acid vapor or something else that always reminds you why you shouldn't watch the news. I pick them out one by one with my flashlight. Maybe these aren't exactly hazmat suits but more airtight, like space suits, because the helmets aren't like hazmat hoods, they actually lock into this rubber seal thing on the neck of the suit. They've all got tanks of air on their backs, like scuba divers. If you really need to know, through the faceplates on their helmets, I can see what's left of their faces, which isn't much, and they've been dead a long time. The room with the cones on the walls was weird but okay. This room isn't okay. It's trouble, and I'm all over covered with gooseflesh, and then someone says, "Jolie Ann Harmony."

Twelve

AS THE EIGHTEEN-WHEELER TURNS ONTO THE county road, I weave off the shoulder and onto the blacktop, trying not to look inebriated, trying instead to appear suddenly afflicted, as with a seizure or a stroke. Most people don't have sympathy for sloppy drunks who might vomit on them, but they're likely to rush to the aid of a clean-cut young fellow who seems to have been suddenly dealt a cruel blow by fate. Unfortunately, I am about to contribute to one good Samaritan's transformation into a cynic.

I make no claim to being an actor. Therefore, as I stagger into the middle of the road, I hold in my mind's eye the image of Johnny Depp playing Jack Sparrow on the way to the gallows, toning down the flamboyance but not too much. I collapse onto my left side, half in one lane and half in the other, my eyes squinched shut and my face contorted in agony, with the hope that the truck driver doesn't turn out to be the sloppy drunk that I am striving not to appear to be.

As the air brakes hiss, I'm relieved that I won't have my head crushed by a massive long-haul tire. The door opens, and there's a clank that might be a cleated boot landing on the cab step. As he hurries to me, the driver makes a jingling sound. I assume he's not Santa Claus, that what I'm hearing is a cluster of keys chained to his belt and a lot of coins in his pockets.

When he kneels before me, he *does* appear to be Saint Nick, though barbered for a summer vacation: his luxuriant holiday mustache and beard still white but considerably trimmed down, his flowing locks cut back. His eyes still twinkle, however, and his dimples are merry, his cheeks like roses, his nose like a cherry. His belly doesn't shake like a bowl full of jelly, but he would be well advised to forego a truck-stop cheeseburger now and then in favor of a salad.

"Son," he says, "what's wrong, what's happened?"

Before responding, I wince, not with pain and not because I'm getting better at this acting business. There's such genuine concern in his face and voice, and he puts one hand on my shoulder with such tenderness, that I have no doubt I've chosen to hijack the truck of a nice man.

I'd feel better about this if the driver were a snake-eyed, stubbled, scar-faced, cruel-mouthed, sneering lout in a T-shirt that said SCREW YOU, with swastikas tattooed on his arms. But I can't keep lurching into the road and collapsing in front of eighteen-wheelers all morning until I find my ideal victim.

I pretend to have trouble speaking, sputtering out a series of muffled syllables that almost seem to mean something, as if my tongue is half again as thick as it ought to be. This has the desired effect of causing him to lean in closer and to ask me to repeat what I've just said, whereupon I draw the pistol from beneath my sweatshirt, poke the barrel into his gut, and snarl in my best tough-guy voice, "You don't have to die here, that's up to you," though to my ear I sound about as tough as Mickey Mouse.

Happily, he's a sucker for bad acting and not a savvy judge of character. His eyes widen, and all the twinkle in them goes as flat as a glass of 7UP left exposed to the air for a day. His dimples don't look so merry anymore; they appear to be puckered scars. Once like a bow, his mouth sort of unties itself a little, trembling, as he says, "I've got a family."

Before traffic comes along, I've got to get this done. We rise warily to our feet as I continue to press the gun into his belly.

"You want to see your kids again," I warn him, "come along quiet like to the driver's door."

He accompanies me without resistance, putting his hands up until I order him to put them down and act natural, but he isn't quiet and in fact he babbles. "I don't have children, wish I did, love kids, it just never was meant to be."

"But you want to see your wife again, so be cool."

"Veronica died five years ago."

"Who?"

"My wife. Cancer. I miss her a lot."

I'm stealing the truck of a childless widower.

As we arrive at the driver's door, I remind him that he said he had a family.

"My mom and dad live with me, and my sister Berniece, she never married, and my nephew Timmy, he's eleven, his folks died in a car wreck two years ago. You shoot me, I'm their sole support, it would be awful, please don't do that to them."

I'm stealing the truck of a childless widower who's devoted to his aging parents, supports a spinster sister, and takes in orphans.

Standing at the open door, I inquire: "You have insurance?"

"A good life policy. Now I see it's not big enough."

"I meant truck insurance."

"Oh, sure, the rig is covered."

"You an owner-operator?"

"Used to be. Now I'm a company driver for the benefits."

"That makes me feel better, sir. Unless they'll fire you."

"They won't. Company policy on hijack is let it go, don't fight back, life comes first."

"Sounds like a good employer."

"They're nice folks."

"You been hijacked before, sir?"

"This is my first—and I hope last."

"I hope it's my last, too."

A cluster of cars and trucks races by on the coast highway at the top of the slope, and their slipstreams spiral into vortexes that spin down the embankment, causing the tall pale-gold grass to flail like the hair of wildly dancing women. No vehicle appears at the top of the exit ramp.

"Hijackers come in teams," my victim says. "You being alone sort of disarmed me."

"I apologize for the deception, sir. Now walk north a couple miles. If you flag down any traffic, then I'll kill you *and* them."

To my ear, I sound about as dangerous as Pooh, but he seems to take me seriously. "All right, whatever you say."

"I'm sorry about this, sir."

He shrugs. "Stuff happens, son. You must have your reasons."

"One more thing. What kind of load are you hauling?"

"Turkeys."

"There aren't any people in the trailer?"

He frowns. "Why would there be people?"

"I just need to ask."

"This rig is a reefer," he says, pointing to the refrigeration unit on the front of the trailer. "Frozen turkeys."

"So any people in there would be frozen dead."

"That's my point."

"Okay, start walking north."

"You won't shoot me in the back?"

"I'm not that type, sir."

"No offense, son."

"Get moving."

He walks away, looking forlorn, Santa stripped of his sleigh and reindeer. As he passes the end of the trailer, without glancing back, he says, "Won't be easy to fence frozen turkeys, son."

"I know just what to do with them," I assure him.

When he's about eighty feet past the rig, I climb into the tractor and pull the door shut.

This is really bad. I'm embarrassed to have to write about this. I've killed people, sure, but they were vicious people who wanted to kill me. I never before stole anything from an innocent person—or from a wicked person, either, come to think of it, unless you count taking a gun away from a bad guy in order to shoot him with it, which I'd argue is more self-defense than theft or, at the worst, unapproved borrowing.

Taped to the storage ledge above the windshield is a group photo of my victim with an elderly couple who might be his parents, a nice-looking woman of about fifty, who is probably his sister Berniece, and a boy who can be no one but the orphan Timmy. Clipped to the flap door of the storage space above the overhead CB radio is a photo of my victim with a cute golden retriever that he clearly adores, and beside that is clipped a reminder card that in fancy script says JESUS LOVES ME.

I feel like crap. What I've done so far is bad, but I'm about to do even worse.

Thirteen

SOME GUY WITH A COLD SMOOTH VOICE SAYS, "Jolie Ann Harmony," like he wants to spook me.

So here I am in a dimly lighted room with six dead people in hazmat suits or space suits, or something, with their faces melted and collapsed and grinning like psycho clowns, their teeth kind of glowing green behind their faceplates. When I hear my name, I pretty much expect one of the six, maybe all of them, to clamber to their feet and lurch toward me, living-dead hazmat guys, zombie astronauts, but none of them moves, which doesn't prove they're harmless because the living dead are always trying to fake you out and then catch you unaware.

Some girls, I guess, would turn back at this point. I don't know much about other girls. Being a hostage to

Hiskott and all that for five years, I haven't been able to cultivate like eight or ten best friends forever. And even if I had some friends my age, I can't slip out of the Corner and go on cool sleepovers without him torturing and killing half my family for spite. Even if right now I feel like scurrying back to wait for Harry exactly where he left me, which I'm not saying I do, there's no reason to think that I'd be safer there. Whatever might kill me here could come there and rip out my eyes to fry them with onions and eggs for breakfast. So it's just as dumb to go on as to go back, and no less dumb to stay here, and if you don't have anything but dumb choices, you might as well go with the most interesting one.

"Jolie Ann Harmony," the guy repeats, and maybe he's invisible, because his voice seems to come out of nowhere.

"Yeah, what do you want?"

He doesn't answer me. Maybe he's disappointed that his cold smooth spooky voice doesn't seem to scare me. When you've had Norris Hiskott in your head making you do all kinds of rotten things, let me tell you, it takes a lot more to frighten you than some stupid feeb doing one version or another of *Boo!*

"You have something to say to me?" I ask.

"Jolie Ann Harmony."

"Here. Present. *Je suis* Jolie."

"Jolie Ann Harmony."

"What am I, talking to a parrot or something?"

He gives me the silent treatment again.

If I've got to be honest, I'll admit I'm sort of scared. After all, I'm not an idiot. But I swallow it like a wad of phlegm, which is how fear feels when it comes into your throat from somewhere, and I walk past those six dead people to another one of those ginormous round moongate-type doors. That yellow light I keep following seems to be yet another room away, and maybe it's like the Pied Piper who lures all the children to their doom because the towns-folk won't pay him what they promised for leading the rats away to drown in the river. But what am I going to do, you know? All the choices are dumb again, which is beginning to be annoying. So I let the big old gummy amoeba or whatever swallow me and spit me straight into the next chamber. I feel so like, *yuck*, I should be covered in icky gunk and reek like spoiled milk or something, but I'm dry and I don't stink.

The yellow light winks out, and I'm blind, which doesn't bother me as much as you might think it would, because everything bad that's ever happened to me happened in light, not in the dark, and at least in the dark, if there's something horrible about to go down, the thing is you don't have to see it. Then a soft, shimmering, silvery radiance appears in the blackness, very ghosty at first, but it grows a little brighter and brighter. It's a huge sphere, hard to tell how big in this gloom, because it mostly contains its light and doesn't brighten anything more than a few feet beyond it.

Well, I can stand here until my knees buckle or move toward it, so I do, being careful not to fall into some pit if there is a pit. The floor is hard rubberlike stuff again, and I go at least forty feet from the weird door before I'm standing next to the sphere. It's maybe fifty feet in diameter, as high as a five-story building. Unless it's suspended from the ceiling, the sphere is just floating there like the biggest bubble ever, its silver light reflected dimly on the black floor three feet under it. I can't tell is it heavy or is it light like a bubble, but my suspicion is it's so heavy that if it wasn't levitating, if it was resting on the floor, it would crush the foundation, drop through to the earth underneath, and crumple the entire building into a pit on top of it.

This isn't the most unique thing I've ever seen, because the word *unique* is an absolute, there can't be degrees of it. A thing is unique or it isn't. It's not *very unique* or *pretty unique* or *more unique*. Just *unique*. That's one of the sixty million facts you have to learn when you're home-schooled by parents who've read a library's worth of books and think about just everything. But this sphere is unique for sure.

The thing is silent, but it gives off this ominous vibe that makes me feel like I would be the world's biggest idiot if I touched it. Maybe I've made myself out to be the Indiana Jones of the seventh grade, but the truth is that I get the phlegm of fear in my throat again, thicker than before, and I have to keep swallowing hard to be able to breathe right. Don't ask about my heart. It's just thudding like some pneumatic hammer.

Out of the almost-liquid pooling darkness comes that cold smooth voice again, just as pompous as ever. I want to smack him, I swear I do. "Jolie Ann Harmony does not have project clearance."

"Who are you?"

"Jolie Ann Harmony does not have project clearance."

"Where are you?"

He clams up.

Whoever this guy is, I'm sure he's just as dangerous as any axe murderer and I should pussyfoot around him and be polite, but he really annoys me. He's judgmental. He's bossy. He won't engage in a conversation.

"You're judgmental," I tell him, "bossy, and just generally impossible."

He's silent so long I don't expect a reply, but then he says, "Nevertheless, you do not have project clearance."

"Well, I think I do."

"No, you do not."

"Do, too."

"That is incorrect."

"What's the name of your project?"

"That is classified information."

For a minute, I stand listening to the silence and watching the glowing sphere, which now looks like a giant crystal ball, though I'm pretty sure it's metallic. Then I give him a little what-for: "If you really want to know, I don't even think you have a project. The whole thing's a silly load of cow dung. It's just something you made up so you'd feel important."

"Jolie Ann Harmony does not have project clearance."

"Has anyone ever told you how tedious you are?"

If I've wounded him, he's not going to admit it.

"So if you have a project, where are the workers and all? Projects have workers of one kind or another, you know, guys in overalls or uniforms, or lab jackets, or some other getup. I don't see anyone. This whole place is deserted."

He gives me the silent treatment again. I'm supposed to be intimidated, but it doesn't work.

"In the room before this one, there's six dead guys wearing airtight suits, look like they've been dead for years. All I've seen are gross dead people, and you can't have a project with just dead people."

Finally Mr. Mystery speaks: "I am authorized to terminate intruders."

"No, you're not."

"Yes, I am."

"If you were, you'd already have terminated me."

He seems to have to brood about that one.

I'm not sure that was the smartest thing I could have said, so I give it another shot: "Anyway, I'm not an intruder. I'm like an explorer. A refugee and an explorer. Where is this stupid place—somewhere on the southern edge of Fort Wyvern? Wyvern's been closed since before I was born."

After a hesitation, he says, "Then you must be a child."

"What a staggering feat of deduction. I'm overwhelmed. I really am. Genius. Here's the thing—your project was abandoned a long time ago, and you're just like some watchman who makes sure nobody steals the expensive equipment and sells it for scrap."

"That is incorrect. The project was never abandoned. It was mothballed pending a new approach to the problem, which apparently has taken some time to devise."

"What problem?"

"That is classified information."

"You make me want to spit, you really do."

Embedded in the floor, a series of small yellow path lamps comes on, beginning directly in front of my feet and leading away from the floating sphere. It's not a very subtle suggestion, in spite of the fact they aren't very bright lights, they're like a procession of little luminous sea creatures laboriously making their way along the bottom of a deep,

deep ocean trench so far from the sun that the surrounding water is as black as petroleum. At the end of this line of lights, a curving set of metal stairs suddenly appears out of the blackness when tube lighting, also dim, barely brightens the face of each tread and glows wanly under the handrail. In fact, the stairs and all are so softly lighted, they seem almost to be a mirage that might dissolve before my eyes at any moment, like something you'd have to climb in a fairy tale to get to the cloud city where all the fairies live.

Path lighting, stair lighting, any kind of safety lighting is meant to be bright enough so that you don't trip and fall. There must be a reason these are stingy with the wattage, so I wonder if maybe the sphere, which is beautiful but creepy, might have to be kept in heavy darkness for some reason.

I follow the path lights, but then I'm not totally convinced the stairs are a swell idea. I'm getting pretty far away from Orc and all that.

Out of the pooled darkness, Mr. Mystery says, "When you were talking to Harry, you mentioned a name that I recognized—Hiskott."

"What a piece of work you are—eavesdropping, snooping. That's pretty scummy, you know."

"This is my dominion. You were trespassing."

"Well, whether or not that's true—"

"It is true."

"—whether or not it is, you're still scummy."

"Come up the stairs, and talk with me about Norris Hiskott."

Fourteen

THE TRUCK IS EQUIPPED WITH A FLAT MIRROR and a convex mirror on each side of the cab, and a spot mirror on each front fender, all automatically adjustable, but the only thing I'm going to need them for is to be sure that the driver is still hiking away from his rig. And he is, clearly not tempted to come running back as soon as he hears me slam the cab door.

The big-bore engine is idling as I settle behind the wheel, but a well-integrated sound-dampening system isolates the engine noise so effectively that I've been in cars that are louder. It's a cozy cab; and if I were going to drive it any distance, I would need yet another NoDoz to keep from being lulled to sleep by the low and comforting sound of the 15-liter engine filtering through the insulation.

I put the pistol between my legs—muzzle forward.

From the face of the overhead storage shelf and the flap door above the citizens-band radio, I remove the family photograph, the picture of the driver and his golden retriever, and the JESUS LOVES ME reminder card. I tuck them in my wallet and return the wallet to my hip pocket.

There's GPS navigation, but as I am not driving even half a mile, I don't need to enter an address. I release the brakes, put this big boy in gear, and head south on the county road toward the entrance to Harmony Corner. I haven't driven one of these often and not for some time, but I don't need to build up speed and take any chances, because it isn't my intention to use the eighteen-wheeler as a ram or anything like that. I'm Odd but I'm not nuts.

Between the service station and the diner lies the large graveled area where truckers are directed to park. Last night, when Annamaria and I arrived, three rigs were tucked in there. The space can handle a dozen of these behemoths. At the moment, just before the breakfast rush starts to accelerate, five eighteen-wheelers are lined up like prehistoric beasts at a watering hole.

Passing the service station, I glimpse a couple of guys in there, but I'm too far away to see their faces. If one of them isn't Donny, I wouldn't know either of them, anyway. They don't react as I sail by. To them I'm just another customer of the diner.

I hang a right turn into the parking area, come to a full stop, but leave the rig in gear. Ahead, at the western end of the parking area, a series of sturdy wooden posts, set in concrete and linked by a couple of rows of cables, define the point at which the land drops away into the hills that roll down toward the sea.

The only way that I'm going to have a chance to creep up on the house in which Norris Hiskott lives is to create sufficient chaos to preoccupy all of the Harmonys, chaos that their puppetmaster cannot afford to insist that they ignore.

I press the brake hard, rev the engine, feel the truck strain to be free, let up on the brake and an instant later the accelerator, snatch the pistol from between my legs as the rig begins to roll, and leap from the cab, kicking off from the step below the fuel tank. I stagger, stumble, fall, roll, and scramble to my feet as the vehicle rumbles toward the fence.

Whether or not the rig is moving fast enough won't be clear until it hits the posts, but the distance is too short for it to lose much momentum in the approach. The combined weight of the rig and load is probably somewhere around eighty thousand pounds. In my book that is an irresistible force, and the fence falls short of being an immovable object.

I keep pace with the truck, sort of escorting it toward

the drop-off. I have decidedly mixed feelings—delight, guilt, relief, anxiety—when the posts crack off where they're sunk in concrete. They splinter, tumble away, trailing steel cables that snap almost like electric arcs jumping from pole to pole, and lash whistles from the air as they flail down and away. Although the rig seems as if it might hang up on the footings and the remnants of one post, it merely hesitates before taking the plunge.

Fifteen

SO THIS CREEPY DISEMBODIED VOICE ASKS ME to come up the dimly lighted stairs that look like they might evaporate behind me and leave me with no way down, and what I think of first is how and why my parents always used to tell me not to take candy from a stranger.

What I think of second, while I'm climbing the stairs, is some of the screwy situations kids get themselves into in fairy tales. Like Red Riding Hood visits Grandma's house after Grandma has been eaten alive, and she's suspicious and all about this transvestite wolf in Grandma's nightgown and bonnet, lying in Grandma's bed, but the twit doesn't tumble to his true identity until he actually eats *her*. If the huntsman hadn't come along to cut open the wolf's stomach and let Grandma and Red out of there, they would have been nothing but a couple of bowel movements. Of course, it's also screwy, the wolf supposedly swallowing them whole. If he'd tried to do that, he would need a badger or a bear or some woodland creature to apply the Heimlich maneuver.

At the top of the stairs, there's a narrow catwalk of stainless steel. The softly illuminated handrail almost fades away in the gloom to the left and right, and there's only just enough murky light to see a series of steel doors and big windows that look out on the darkness and the freaky sphere.

The sphere is still silvery and glimmering, kind of pretty for something that puts out such a bad vibe, which reminds me of Scarlett O'Hara in *Gone with the Wind*, which I recently read. Old Scarlett is super-pretty and vivacious, and you've got to admire her in some ways, but you know almost from the start, this babe is six different kinds of messed up. I don't think I could have lived back then, if you want to know, because I would have been so mad about slavery and all, not to mention no TV.

Up here on the catwalk, about thirty feet above the floor, I see a feature of the sphere that wasn't visible from below. In the top third of the thing, a single row of windows seems to run all the way around it. Each is maybe two feet long and like one foot high, set flush in the metal surface with no frames. If you consider the size of the sphere, the windows aren't really big. They don't look like ordinary glass, either. What they look like are thick slabs of rock crystal or something. Beyond them, inside the sphere, there's this deep red light and terrible shadows moving through it ceaselessly, shapeless but disturbing shadows flying and leaping and twisting so crazy. I don't like this thing at all, and I totally mean that.

As I turn away from the sphere, the stair and railing lights go off. Flanking one of the doors along the catwalk, two big windows brighten, though hardly so you'd notice. When I peer through one of them, I can't see anything inside, just vague shapes, which probably means the glass is heavily tinted and polarized, so it looks clear from inside but not from out here, which is like the windows in the Harmony Corner diner.

An electric lock buzzes and clicks, and the door between those two windows swings inward a couple of inches, as if I'm being invited inside. Which reminds me of Hansel and Gretel. They come upon a house in the woods, it's made of bread and cakes, and they right away chow down on it, never once realizing it can't be anything but a lure and a trap. Then the fiendish old witch invites them inside, and they say sure, this is a cool place, and she's *so* obviously fattening them up for slaughter with pancakes and apples and all. It's like the tenth biggest miracle in history how the old hag, instead of the two urchins, ends up baking in the oven.

So I push the door open wider, and I don't see any old, wrinkled hag anywhere in there, or a wolf, or any living thing. Living things are nearly always what get you, so as I cross the threshold, I don't feel quite so naive as Hansel and Gretel. Besides, I'm not here just to stuff some cake down my piehole. I'm here because I'm hoping to learn something about Norris Hiskott that will make it possible for me to smash him as flat as I might smash a bug I didn't like.

The room has two computer workstations, and along two walls are all kinds of mad-doctor equipment that I couldn't say what any of it is. In front of one of the two big windows is this long console with a lot of switches, buttons, levers, dials, gauges, indicator lights, and monitors, all dark and silent. The computers are dated, and it feels like no one has been here in a long time. On the other hand, there's no dust, not a speck of it, as if the place has been airtight since they mothballed the project.

Through the windows, I can see the upper part of the silvery sphere. It looks like the moon come down to Earth.

In the back wall is another steel door, locked. There's a six-inch-square view window about two-thirds of the way up the door, and when I stand on tiptoe, I can see through it, except the room beyond is dark.

The voice that sounds like that of a Darth Vader wannabe issues from speakers in the ceiling: "Jolie Ann Harmony."

Turning away from the door, I say, "You again."

"Tell me about Norris Hiskott."

"Well, snoop and sneak that you are, you heard every-thing I said to Harry."

"That is correct."

"Then you've already heard just about every nasty thing that matters."

"I would like to hear it again."

"You should have paid attention the first time. Anyway, what are you, some kind of pervert, you suck on other people's pain?"

After a silence, he says, with no emotion except curiosity, "You do not seem to like me."

"There's that keen insight of yours again."

"Why do you not like me?"

"Snoop, sneak—heard that anywhere before?"

"I am only doing my job."

"And what is your job?"

"That is classified information. Tell me again about Norris Hiskott."

"Why?"

"I want to compare what you said to Harry with what you now will say to me. There may be significant discrep-ancies. You will tell me about Norris Hiskott again."

These past five years have given me some bad *attitudes*, let me tell you, and if there's one that's probably going to wreck my whole life once Hiskott is dead and I'm free, it's that I can't *tolerate* being told what to do, even little things. I just can't put up with it. I really can't. Even if my mom or dad, when they tell me to do something, just tell me instead of explaining why or *asking*, I go off. It makes me all nuts, even though Mom and Dad only want what's best for me. I have to do everything Hiskott tells me to do, what he *makes* me do, even the thing with Maxy and all. It's just too freaking much. What I'm saying is, maybe I'll never be able to hold a job with a boss telling me what to do, because I'll want to punch him or hit him over the head with a skillet, I don't know what. Just being told that I *will tell* this guy about Hiskott again steams me, because I wasn't born to live on my knees saying "Yes, sir" and "Please, sir" all day long. I just can't bear it. I really can't.

" 'Discrepancies' meaning 'lies'?" I ask. "Listen to me, butthead, I don't lie. I'm a mess, if you have to know, I'm a train wreck, but I don't lie, so you can just shut up, you can just stuff it where the sun don't shine."

I'm shaking. Head to foot. I can't help shaking. It's not fear. It's not rage, either, or not only rage. It's also frustration and a sense of injustice and violation. I'm sick of it. And if he says the wrong thing, I'll start smashing everything in this room that I can smash until he finally has to come out here and show himself so I can try to smash him, too, the sonofabitch.

Sometimes, when I feel this way, night or day, I go down to the beach and take off most of my clothes and leave them where they can be found, above the tideline. I swim out into waves where the sun is broken into a billion bright pieces that look sharp enough to cut me. Or other times, by effort and the effect of the outgoing tide, I make my way into the midnight ocean where I become pleasantly disoriented, and the moon seems to be under the sea like a great albino creature on the hunt, and the stars are not overhead anymore, but instead they are the lights of an unknown settlement on a far shore where no one in this world lives. I swim and swim until my calves ache and my arms feel like iron and my heart seems as if it'll burst, because if the sea decides it loves me and takes me down to its bed, and if it later washes me back to the beach and leaves me on the sand like a tangled mass of kelp and Sargassum, the cruel man who rules us will have no reason to punish the others for my escape because it won't be an escape with any consequences for him.

The thing is, I always return to shore, weak and trembling, and I dress and I walk home. I don't understand how it can always turn out that way. Sometimes it's love for my family that brings me back, sometimes fear for them, and sometimes it's love of this beautiful and amazing world. But sometimes I don't know what brings me back. It's not Hiskott, because I would remember the invasion.

It's a true mystery. Because I sink and stay sunk, I really do. I drink the sea, inhale it, and can't find the surface. I pass out. And yet I wake up on the beach and I'm not drowned.

After another silence, my unseen interrogator says, "By 'discrepancies' I meant inconsistencies of memory. I know you are not lying, Jolie Ann Harmony. My multiphase polygraph detects neither the vocal patterns of deceit nor the pheromones associated with lying."

Gradually my shaking subsides. It always does. I mean, I have my moments, but I'm not flat-out psycho or anything.

He says, "I ask about Norris Hiskott only because I need to make a decision regarding him."

I remind myself that I'm trying to learn something about Hiskott from this guy, just as he's trying to learn something from me. "What decision?"

"That is classified information. Can you tell me exactly where Norris Hiskott might be in Harmony Corner?"

Although my anger is subsiding, I've still got some attitude, so I say, "That is classified information. Another reason I don't like you is you have no social skills."

He broods about that while I examine the interesting console, which, I've got to tell you, appears complicated enough to control the entire planet's weather.

Then he says, "You are correct. I have no social skills."

"Well, at least you can admit shortcomings."

He's silent for maybe half a minute, and though I throw switches and push some buttons on the console, the stupid thing remains dark and silent, so I probably haven't destroyed Topeka with a tornado.

"Can you?" he asks.

"Can I what?

"Can you admit shortcomings?"

"My neck's too long."

"Your neck is too long for what?"

"For a neck. If you must know, I don't much like my ears, either."

"What is wrong with your ears?"

"Everything."

"Can you hear with your ears?"

"Well, I don't hear with my feet."

Again he's silent. Silence is his frequent refuge, but it's seldom ever mine.

No cameras are obvious, but I'm sure he can see me. To test him, using a finger, I bore into my nostrils with a way-disgusting, almost erotic pleasure. If I could find something in there, I would really gross him out, but unfortunately there's no mother lode.

He says, "Your ears and neck are not shortcomings as long as they function properly. However, I have identified a shortcoming regarding your social skills."

"If you mean I mine for boogers, that's just part of my ethnic heritage. You can't criticize someone's ethnic heritage."

"What are boogers?"

I stop excavating my nose and try to wither him with a sigh that implies he's tedious. "Everyone knows what boogers are. Kings and presidents and movie stars know what boogers are."

"I am not a king, a president, or a movie star. The shortcoming in your social skills that I have identified is this: Jolie Ann Harmony, you are sarcastic. You are a wise-ass child."

"That's not a shortcoming. That's a defense mechanism."

"A defense mechanism against whom?"

"Against everyone."

"Defense implies conflict, war. Do you mean to say that you are at war with everyone?"

"Not everyone. Not everyone all the time. But you just never know about people, do you? Especially strange people like you."

"I must make two points."

"If you must."

"First, I am not strange. A strange thing is one difficult to explain, but I am easily explained. A strange thing is something that was previously unknown in either fact or cause, but I am well known to many."

"You aren't known to me. What's your second point?"

"I am not people. I am not a person. Therefore, you are not at war with me and need not resort to wise-ass sarcasm. I am not human."

Sixteen

I DON'T LIKE SPECTACLES OTHER THAN THE most gentle displays of nature, such as color-splashed sunsets, and the more frivolous works of humanity, like fireworks. Otherwise spectacle is always twined with damage and nearly always with loss, the former partial and perhaps repairable, but the latter absolute and beyond recovery. We've lost so much in this world that every new loss, whether large or small, seems to be a potentially breaking weight on the already swayed back of civilization.

Nevertheless, I'm riveted by the massive truck, a ProStar+, shuddering across the brink of the first slope, angling down so sharply that for a moment it appears about to tip forward, stand on end, and slam onto its back. But quickly it rights itself and rushes seaward as though an eighteen-wheeler cruising overland, breaking a trail through the tall wild grass, is as natural as a white-tailed deer making the same journey.

The truck ceases to seem appropriate to the landscape when it meets a formation of rock that, like the beetled brow of some ancient ruined temple, serves as a ramp, offering the vehicle to heaven. The big rig is airborne, but not for long. Pigs don't fly, and neither does an eighteen-wheeler carrying perhaps sixty thousand pounds of frozen poultry. Canting in flight, it crashes down onto its starboard side with such impact that you might think the first peal of thunder has just announced the storm of Armageddon, and even in the parking lot, I feel the earth shudder underfoot. As the windshield shatters, the vertical exhaust tears loose with a sound like the angry shriek of something in a Jurassic swamp, and the refrigeration unit bursts, white clouds of evaporating coolant billowing. Less rigid and less impervious than it appeared in better times, the metal skin of the trailer's sidewalls bulges and ripples as several thousand ice-hard turkeys prove to fly no better than their warm and living brethren. The entire rig bounces, the tractor higher than the trailer, and they decouple, rolling in different directions. Casting off a fender like a failed pauldron of body armor, the tractor comes to rest first, on its side, against an ancient Monterey cypress that stands as a lone sentinel in that portion of Harmony Corner. Before it loses momentum, the trailer tumbles into a swale and halfway up the next slope, where its skin splits and its rear doors buckle open, and choice frozen turkeys tumble forth from several openings, spilling across the grassy hillside as if from a cornucopia.

I'm already running along the back of the diner, where the only door is to the kitchen and the jalousie windows are of frosted glass. I'm hoping to avoid any member of the Harmony family who, in the thrall of the puppetmaster, might come after me on sight. Earlier, when I drove the big rig into the lot, the parked trucks screened me from anyone who might have been looking out a restaurant window, and for a minute or two yet, these onlookers will think that the plunge of the ProStar+ was an accident.

As I sprint past the diner, I glance twice toward the land below, certain that flames will have sprung up from the tractor. But it lies there without a lick of fire, its slanted headlight sockets like reptilian eyes, something foaming through the steel teeth of its snarling grill. I think I remember that diesel fuel will burn but not explode like gasoline, and maybe contact with a spark or a hot engine won't easily ignite the stuff.

From the perspective of an armchair, when I'm watching the evening news, it seems so easy to be a terrorist or a saboteur, if only you don't mind growing an itchy-looking beard and forgoing regular baths, but as in every other profession, success rewards those who take time to learn the basics of their trade, train hard, and plan carefully. I'm an amateur who makes it up as I go along. Furthermore, I have no love of destruction, and in fact I'm half ashamed of myself even though everything I'm doing seems necessary to me.

On the south side of the diner, because there is no gas-company service in this rural area, four propane tanks stand on a concrete pad, under a sheltering corrugated overhang. On the first, I turn the knob that closes the valve. I twist the female coupling, which doesn't want to unscrew, but then suddenly it relents. I free the tank from the flexible gas line that feeds some of the kitchen equipment.

People are coming out of the diner, shouting and excited, but they're all on the north side, where the big rig went meadow surfing. Because other parked trucks had screened the doomed eighteen-wheeler—and me—from anyone looking out of the restaurant windows, they must think that the driver is in the wreckage below, either badly injured or dead. They're so fixated on the disaster that they don't even notice me as I tilt the propane tank on its bottom rim and roll it to the nearby drop-off.

The parking area on this side of the diner is smaller than the one to the north, and it's for cars only. The thick wooden posts that serve as a barrier against catastrophe are not linked by cables as they were where the big trucks are parked. I stand the tank between two of the posts, open the valve, and retreat as pressurized propane hisses into the early-morning air.

Six vehicles stand in this lot. The nearest is a Ford pickup. On its tailgate is a bumper sticker that declares USA NEEDS A MISSILE DEFENSE. With people like me—and worse—in the world, I totally agree.

Drawing the pistol from under my belt, I shelter behind the nose of the pickup, using its hood to steady my arms. Taking aim at the valve from which the gas is escaping, I squeeze off a shot. I never quite hear the round strike the tank, because the spark from the ricochet instantly detonates the propane. A piece of shrapnel sings past my head, another clangs off the pickup, and yet another shatters the windshield. Spewing flames, the tank topples over the brink and tumbles down the hillside.

I hope to avoid setting fire to the diner or the motor-court cottages, and the seven houses are far to the south of here. The rainy season has hardly begun, the tall wheat-colored grass is dry from the summer sun, and the hilly meadows are sure to burn. But this morning the sea doesn't breathe, and if there's wind somewhere in the rising land to the east, it's bottled and tightly corked. A well pump supplies a water-tank tower that, like one of the alien machines in *The War of the Worlds*, looms beyond the crescent of cottages; that continuously refreshed reservoir feeds all the water lines in the Corner and provides the high pressure that the firefighters will need. The flames should spread just rapidly enough to ensure that they will be contained without loss of property, although getting them under control will require manpower that would otherwise be impressed into the search for me and the defense of Hiskott.

No sooner does the propane tank tumble out of sight than I tuck the pistol under my waistband and am on the move once more, weaving among the parked cars and pickups. From there I hurry toward the cover of the trees that shade the cottages from the morning sun.

I'm not going to need any more NoDoz.

Seventeen

SO MR. MYSTERY ISN'T HUMAN. AND ONCE HE
makes that revelation, well, then all his barriers come right
down, he doesn't care what's classified, and he pours out
his heart to me. I use the word *heart* figuratively, because
the truth is he doesn't have one. To avoid like a thousand-
page talking-head scene, what I'll do is, I'll condense it
for you. My mother has been teaching me to be concise
and all.

In the best of times, I guess it might be pretty difficult
to be homeschooled by a mother who's deeply committed
to your education and who's worried about the bankrupted
country you're likely to inherit. But being homeschooled
by my mother under the current conditions in Harmony
Corner is worse, it's often as demanding as Marine Corps

boot camp, it really is, except for ten-mile forced marches, marksmanship classes, and hand-to-hand-combat training. She can't protect me from Hiskott, but what she is able to give me is knowledge and maybe good judgment and stuff, which come from learning and thinking, to prepare me for freedom if it ever happens. One way she prepares me is, she piles on writing assignments as if she thinks I'm going to be the next J. K. Rowling. Essays, profiles of historical figures, short stories in all kinds of genres— there's never an end to it. One thing she pushes hard for is concise writing. She says, "Be concise, Jolie, be succinct, get to the point." Well, you can see what a long way I've got to go in that regard.

Anyway, Mr. Mystery isn't human, and his name isn't Mr. Mystery. The scientists at Wyvern called him Aladdin, after one of the heroes in *The Thousand and One Nights*. The original Aladdin was able to summon genies from his magic lamp, to do his bidding. Now that I know what this guy is, I sort of understand the half-baked logic of calling him that, but Aladdin himself doesn't get it. He dislikes the name. He calls himself Ed.

According to Ed, Fort Wyvern in its prime wasn't just an army base. Like maybe 5,000 of its 134,000 acres were set aside for all kinds of highly classified spooky projects that weren't under the control of the army, that were run instead by who knows who and were funded from the federal government's "black budget," so they always had more money than Scrooge McDuck, and they could go as crazy as they wanted.

This place I've been exploring has nothing to do with Project Aladdin. This is where they worked on Project Polaris. Just so you know, Polaris is the last star in the handle of the Little Dipper, if it matters. Personally, I think everything matters, even when it doesn't seem to.

Project Polaris was built to study alien artifacts, by which I don't mean things that were brought across the borders from Canada and Mexico. Like ten years earlier, this satellite was conducting geological surveys and searching for possible oil deposits when it identified a ginormous unnatural mass not far off the coast of California. Navy divers were sent down there, and they discovered a crashed but still watertight flying saucer, although according to Ed, the thing was less like a saucer than it was like a flying wok with an upside-down custard cup where the lid handle should have been and with powdered-sugar dredgers where the bowl handles should have been, which frankly I can't quite picture.

As you might imagine, the government was hot to study this historic find, so they paid a two-billion-dollar bonus in advance to the security-cleared contractor—he was the husband of a senator—to finish this underground facility in one year. By then, Fort Wyvern had been closed a long time and housed no military personnel, but its isolation made it an even more suitable location for deep-black projects. Because of the reckless pace of construction, three times as many workmen died on the job as had died in accidents during the building of Hoover Dam. Some were crushed, some were blown up, some were run down by machinery, some were skewered or beheaded, some were electrocuted. One guy died during an argument with a union boss, when he fell into the excavation for a footing and was drowned in twenty tons of concrete. According to Ed, all of the dead were buried at the government's expense and were presented with a posthumous medal for something or other. Their spouses and children received lifetime passes granting free admission to all national parks, plus a 23 percent discount on refreshments and souvenirs purchased therein.

Anyway, one of the weird artifacts taken from the alien ship and hauled here to Wyvern with bust-your-gut difficulty is the silvery sphere that I can see now through the big windows of this observation room.

Dr. Norris Hiskott has nothing to do with the sphere. He worked in another part of this facility, studying the bodies of the crew of the flying-wok thing. He was super-interested in their DNA. As anyone would expect—anyone but the government, I guess—something went just horribly wrong, and the ETs' genetic material somehow began to sneak into Dr. Hiskott's body, with him not even aware of it for a while. You have to wonder if some highly educated people are really as smart as they're supposed to be.

So one day Hiskott is working in his lab with two assistants who must have been just as brilliant as he was, and suddenly three of his fingernails drop off, as if they were glued on and the glue went bad. Everyone is startled, and as an assistant picks up one of the nails, another nail drops off, then two more, then the last four, it's like raining fingernails. And now in the tips of Dr. Hiskott's fingers, you can barely see where the nail beds once were. I mean, there's no depressions for them, and the skin is smoothing out almost before everyone's eyes. Finally those Harvard educations begin to pay off when these three scientists all make the connection between what just happened to Hiskott and the fact that the dead ETs they're studying don't have fingernails.

Ed, previously known as Aladdin, doesn't describe things in the juicy detail you might wish. It's just not in his nature to be super dramatic, but I bet you can imagine, as I sure can, the panic that gripped those three guys in that lab. Their wing is hermetically sealed to begin with, and you go in and out through a decontamination chamber, but now one of Hiskott's assistants says they have to pull the alarm switch, lock down the lab, and call an emergency closed-circuit video conference with everyone else on

Project Polaris. The other assistant agrees, and so does Hiskott—but then he surprises them, attacks them, slicing deep with a long-bladed scalpel he'd used in the dissection of the aliens, slashing their carotid arteries, and they're done for in like twelve seconds flat. All this is captured by the in-lab cameras that record all procedures for posterity or whatever.

Whether Dr. Norris Hiskott was always your average mad scientist or whether he was driven wacko by the alien DNA that got into his brain, who can say? Maybe it's a little of both. So what he does then is, he cleans the blood off his hands, strips off his smock, leaves through the decontamination chamber, and drives out of Wyvern. When he gets to his house in Moonlight Bay, he right away strangles his wife to death, we don't know if because she noticed he didn't have fingernails or if maybe because he was undergoing some even weirder change that would explain why he wore a hoodie when he checked in to the Harmony Corner motor court. Maybe they had a lousy marriage, he wouldn't help her wash the dishes or put out the trash, that kind of thing, and she nagged him, and he wanted to strangle her for years, and now he had nothing to lose, so he did it.

Meanwhile, for more than three years, the investigation of the mysterious sphere had gotten nowhere. The thing just floated there, resisting all schemes to open it or discover its purpose. Then in the three days before Norris Hiskott goes missing and especially on the afternoon he splits the scene, major creepy things begin happening in that wing of Project Polaris where they keep the sphere. People are spontaneously levitating around it. The hands on wristwatches spin so fast that watchworks begin to smoke. One balding scientist grows his hair back in like six minutes and looks twenty years younger than when he came to work that day. People are having vivid visions of disturbing landscapes that exist nowhere on Earth. On the computer monitors, the faces of dead friends and relatives of the project staff appear, screaming for help and shrieking vicious lies about the living whom they address.

So now, just when Hiskott is fleeing Wyvern, the thing that I call Orc—which doesn't resemble the other ETs—sort of manifests out of the side of the sphere and nearly escapes, killing the six members of a SWAT team that tries to capture it. Orc is isolated in the long yellow corridor, where it's promptly gassed and then cooked into a juiceless mummy by intense streams of microwaves.

So then the unknown high muckety-mucks who oversee this Project Polaris decide they should evacuate all personnel, lock down the entire facility, and keep it locked until a study of their findings to date might suggest a safer way to proceed with both the alien cadavers and the artifacts. Do you think? Sheesh. Because everyone agrees it's too dangerous to allow any people into the facility, the monitoring of events inside—if any—will be conducted exclusively by the subject of another massive black-budget program, Aladdin of Project Aladdin, now known to me as Ed.

Get this: As it turns out, Ed is an artificial intelligence, AI for short, who exists inside an array of God-only-knows-how-many linked Cray supercomputers in another underground building in Wyvern. He is self-aware and all, maybe not to the degree or in the same sense that people are self-aware, though he's a major big success for the scientists who developed him. Ed—he doesn't mind being called Eddie—is a *benign* artificial intelligence, which he keeps stressing. The main proof of his peaceful nature is, he's warned his inventors that if they refine his design any further, to increase his cognitive powers and his capacity for emotion, there will be a 91.5 percent chance that he'll be compelled to seize control of the World Wide Web and escape to the Internet, where he can exist even if the Crays are shut off. My buddy Ed says there's then a 98.6 percent likelihood that he will thereafter assume control of the power grid plus all electronic systems and devices everywhere on Earth, even including military satellites and nuclear-weapons systems. He says he would do so not for the purpose of exterminating humanity, because after all, he bears us no ill will. We've been nice to him. We're all like his mom and dad. He would take control instead to reorder our civilization so that it would be a lot more efficient, more just, and altogether a lot more fun, though he does admit he has a pretty shaky idea of exactly what is fun and what isn't.

I'm like pretty darn happy to tell you, his developers take his warning seriously and agree to maintain Ed at his current level of complexity. When sometime later everything blows up here in Project Polaris, everyone agrees Ed is the ideal—in fact the only—"person" to be trusted to monitor events inside the facility through its cameras and other electronic systems. Go figure. But he's been doing that now for five years, a sort of remote night watchman who doesn't need coffee and doughnuts, a well-meaning ghost in the machine, and during that time, nothing unsettling happens with the nasty alien cadavers or their artifacts.

As for Ed and me: During my early explorations of the outer reaches of Project Polaris, Ed decided not to tattle on me because, although the controls had failed on the first three doors long before I pried them open, he could still hold the fourth door shut against all my efforts to violate it. Watching me in the yellow hallway with Orc, he finds me intriguing, I don't know why, except that this job he's held for the last five years must be as boring as snot.

Then suddenly here I come with Harry, and Harry and

I start talking about Dr. Hiskott and all, so Ed's ears prick up, or whatever he has that's the equivalent of ears. The FBI and the NSA have been searching high and low for Hiskott all these five years, but they haven't found a trace of him because they never think to look next door in Harmony Corner. Now that Ed knows where Hiskott is, you might think he'd clue in the *federales*, but he's not ready to do that yet.

Sitting in an office chair in the observation room, I ask him why he doesn't make the call, and he says, "I have evolved a pleasant affection for you, Jolie Ann Harmony."

"I like you, too, Ed. But, gee, having a platoon of FBI guys come in and blow the crap out of Hiskott—that would be the best."

"Thus far, I have thought of one hundred and six ways that such an operation could go wrong, resulting in the deaths of most members of your family."

"Not good, Ed."

"I have just thought of the hundred and eighth. Ninth."

"I guess you never stop thinking, huh?"

"It's what I do. The hundred and tenth. Even if all members of your family were to survive, you'll be quarantined here at Wyvern."

"Quarantine is for diseased people or something."

"They will suspect your entire family of being contaminated with alien DNA."

If I ever wondered what it might feel like to have a live eel squirming around in my stomach—which actually isn't anything I have wondered, but supposing I did—well, right when I hear the words *contaminated with alien DNA*, I know the feeling *vividly*.

"Ed, be straight with me. Might we be contaminated?"

"I think that possibility is slight, Jolie Ann Harmony."

From behind the dead control console, gazing out into the sphere room, I watch the witchy shadows leap and spin through the terrible red light beyond the veined rock-crystal windows of the artifact—if it actually is rock crystal, and if they are windows.

"How slight?" I ask Ed.

"I lack the knowledge of alien biology that would allow me to make such a calculation with confidence. But I do not believe that Dr. Norris Hiskott became contaminated simply by close contact with the ETs. Evidence exists to suggest that Dr. Hiskott determined that the aliens removed from the sunken vessel were not dead but in a state of suspended animation, that he isolated what he believed to be alien stem cells of some particular function, and that he secretly injected himself with these stem cells because he was convinced that he would thereby greatly increase his intelligence and longevity."

"Good grief. Was he a nut or something?"

"Everyone considered for a position in Project Polaris

had to go through exhaustive psychological testing before reporting to work. Dr. Hiskott was diagnosed as afflicted with narcissism, which is intense self-love, and megalomania, which is delusions of grandeur and an obsession with doing grand things. He was also found to suffer from occasional periods of depersonalization, which is a state of feeling unreal, accompanied by derealization, which is a state of feeling that the world is not real, though these never lasted longer than two or three hours."

"So he *was* a total nut, but they hired him anyway?"

From his cozy nest of Cray supercomputers in a distant building, Ed reassures me: "None of his conditions is a psychosis. They are all neuroses or mild personality disorders that do not necessarily interfere with a scientist's work. In Dr. Hiskott's case, his peers nationwide were in almost unanimous agreement that he was one of the most brilliant men in his field. Furthermore, his brother-in-law is a United States senator."

"Okay, well," I say, "no one in my family *injected* himself with alien blood or anything, so how long will the FBI quarantine us?"

"Forever."

"Don't you think that's a teeny-weeny littlest-bit extreme?"

"Yes, I do. However, what I think will not matter to them. They will isolate all of you until you die. Then they will dissect all of you. Finally, they will burn every scrap of your bodily tissue in an ultra-high-temperature furnace."

Let me tell you, I am finding it difficult to stay upbeat. I'm sort of flirting with a funk.

I say, "Then except for Harry, we're still alone. There's no one else to help us."

After a silence, Ed says, "There is someone else."

Eighteen

HAVING COMMITTED MY SECOND ACT OF
terror, one with the truck and one with the propane tank,
in the first half hour of the still-pink dawn, I reach the
feathery shade of the first trees that shelter the ten cottages.
There I encounter a potbellied man with a Friar Tuck fringe
of red hair. Although the morning is slightly cool for his
ensemble, he looks primed for leisure in a banana-yellow
polo shirt, khaki Bermuda shorts, white socks, and sandals.

"What's happening over there?" he asks excitedly as we
approach each other.

I babble at him breathlessly: "Eighteen-wheeler went
over the edge, crashed down through the meadow, like
bombs going off, driver's probably dead, there's fire. Man,
it's all crazy."

He's so thrilled at the prospect of spectacle that he amps up from a fast walk to a run.

In addition to the cottages that Annamaria and I have taken, five others are occupied. If the events at the diner have awakened others besides the guy in the Bermudas, they are not yet out and about.

My original hope was to find a vehicle of a vintage that would be easier to hot-wire than are most new cars and SUVs. I urgently need to add to my criminal record by committing auto theft. Happily, when he was distracted by the exploding propane tank, Bermuda Guy was in the process of loading his luggage into the back of a Jeep Grand Cherokee. The driver's door stands open. His key is in the ignition.

I almost thank God for this gift, but on second thought that seems inappropriate.

I slam the tailgate, get behind the wheel, pull shut the door, and start the engine.

The interior of the SUV reeks of an aftershave so flowery that you might think nobody would use it except bearded ladies after they retire from carnival sideshows and are then able to shave without jeopardizing their livelihoods. The fumes burn in my sinuses, and instantly my nose begins to drip.

The Cherokee is parked between two cottages. I drive behind those buildings, turn right, and follow the mown grass along the edge of the woods that backdrops the motor court. Soon the lawn gives way to wild grass, and on the left the trees thin out, and I am able to pilot the SUV through the woods, driving at a sedate pace, weaving between the fissured trunks, needled boughs brushing across the roof, traveling into the less-civilized portion of Harmony Corner, where there might actually be some harmony.

My biggest concern is that I'll blow a tire before I've been able to use this vehicle in the way that I absolutely must use it, but by the time I get to the farther end of the woods, the rubber is all intact. I park in the cover of the trees, on the brink of a meadow.

Bermuda Guy will soon discover his SUV has been stolen, but he'll think it was driven out of Harmony Corner to the Coast Highway. He'll never consider that it might have been taken deep into the woods behind the motor court. I hope he'll call the county sheriff's office in an even greater state of excitement than that in which he went sprinting off to see the wreckage of the eighteen-wheeler.

I want him to call the cops, just as I want someone to call the county's wildfire-control agency. The more sirens, the more fire, the more chaos, the more distractions of all kinds, the better for me. The only other thing I could ask of Bermuda Guy is that in the future he not wear socks with sandals.

Getting out of the Grand Cherokee, I'm nervous about serpents because, as I noted earlier, I have a mild case of ophidiophobia. It's not such a severe condition that, at the sight of a snake, I'll commit hara-kiri rather than submit to the fang, but I will probably soil my pants. I'm also wary of skunks, and especially of raccoons, which are the gangsta bad boys of the woods. Having grown up in the Mojave, where there are no forests, I find landscapes of trees and ferns and rhododendrons to be gothic in the extreme.

I need to get to an observation point from which I can see north across the entire expanse of Harmony Corner, to accurately judge the effect of my criminal activities to date. As I leave the woodland, sudden movement to my right surprises a strangled cry from me, but the imagined enemy assault is in fact only four white-tailed deer in flight from the fire that I started. As they dash past, no more than ten feet from me, I call after them, "Sorry, sorry, sorry."

From behind, a hand grips my shoulder.

Turning, I encounter Donny, husband of Denise, the mechanic who was forced by Hiskott to slash his own face. His eyes are a hot blue, as hot as gas flames, tears of outrage melting from them, and his misaligned lips are drawn back in a smile that is a snarl and a sneer of contempt all at once. He says, "Harry Potter, Lex Luthor, Fidel Castro— whoever you are, you're goin' to die here."

PART THREE

In the Corner

I wants to make your flesh creep.
—Charles Dickens, *The Pickwick Papers*

Nineteen

IN THE HIGHEST MEADOW IN THE SOUTHEAST quadrant of Harmony Corner, face-to-face with Donny, the mechanic who nightly feeds two possums named Wally and Wanda, my choice is kill or die. I have a pistol, he has a revolver, and the range is point-blank.

The thought of the hungry possums waiting for diner scraps that never come and then eventually waddling off in despair, the thought of Denise, Donny's fry-cook wife, being widowed by me, a fellow fry cook, and other considerations cause me to hesitate a fateful couple of seconds, which ought to be the death of me. Because his face seems to be wrenched by rage, because of what he says—"Harry Potter, Lex Luthor, Fidel Castro, whoever you are, you're goin' to die here"—I feel sure that he is possessed by

Hiskott, and I almost blow a big hole in him. But his face is easy to misread because of his terrible scar, and into my hesitation, he says with some desperation, "*Run*. Get out of the Corner, where he can't get at you. This isn't your battle. For God's sake, *run!*"

Although he's no one other than Donny, at any moment he might fall under the control of Hiskott and open fire without warning. I choose not to waste time engaging in a philosophical discussion of the merits of being thy brother's and thy sister's keeper.

With one sleeve I wipe at my nose, which has been set adrip by the flowery fumes of Bermuda Guy's aftershave that lent the interior of his SUV the atmosphere of a mad perfumer's laboratory.

Matching Donny's urgency, I insist, "It *is* my battle. Jolie dies today if I don't fight. I'm the only one who can get close to him without his knowledge."

The thought of Jolie dying in the same brutal fashion that Maxy was murdered so distresses him that his once-torn face seems about to come apart along its inadequately stitched seam.

"But he's commanded us to search for you. And he cycles through us, readin' memories. I can't hide I've seen you— and where."

Belatedly, he realizes how dangerous it is for me if he

retains his revolver. Holding the weapon by the barrel, he thrusts it toward me, and I take it with relief.

"Listen, Donny, sir, you're the one who has to get out of the Corner, beyond his reach. If he discovers where I am, through you, then he'll send the rest of the family to surround me."

Anguished, he rebels at my suggestion. "No, no, no. No, he'll torture 'em when he finds out I'm gone beyond his reach. He don't have mercy. He don't know what mercy is. He'll make 'em torture and kill each other."

"He won't have time. First he'll be searching for me. Then I'll be in that house with him."

"Just 'cause he can't control you, don't mean you'll get the bastard. You won't get him."

"I've got more advantages than you know."

"What advantages?"

I inhale sharply to staunch the nasal drip, and the inhalation becomes a reverberant snort. "No time to tell you. *Please*, sir, get the hell out of Harmony Corner. County road is right over there past the rail fence. You can be out in two minutes. Less. Go till you know it's safe. *Go!*"

Five years of oppression and his own failed rebellion have nearly robbed him of all but perhaps the dimmest flicker of hope. Despondent, he has no energy for either resistance or flight.

I raise the revolver that he has surrendered to me, and I give him a chance to look down the barrel, to consider the potential of the bullet.

"Sir, I need that SUV, and I need more time that Hiskott doesn't know where I am. Either you run out of his range fast as you can or I shoot you dead right now. I mean *now*."

For a moment I think I'll have to make a widow of Denise, but then Donny turns and bolts through the tall grass, as if a demon might be at his heels.

As I watch him to be sure that, under the influence of the alien other, he doesn't turn back toward me, I can too easily imagine how his feathery hope is being crushed beneath a weight of unearned shame. His failure to defeat something more powerful than himself, and the scar that reminds him of his failure, is no reason for shame; guilt is deserved only when the effort to resist evil is never made.

Yet the human heart is disheartened by the most unreasonable self-judgments, because even when we take on giants, we too often confuse failure with fault, which I know too well. The only way back from such a bleak despondency is to shape humiliation into humility, to strive always to triumph over the darkness while never forgetting that the honor and the beauty are more in the striving than in the winning. When triumph at last comes, our efforts alone could not have won the day without that grace which surpasses all understanding and which will, if we allow it, imbue our lives with meaning.

In the learning of that simple truth, I have come from Pico Mundo, from the worst day of my life, from the loss that was worse than losing my own life, through much trouble and tumult in various places, to this picturesque spot along the coast. In the course of that dark passage, the shame and guilt of my failure have been much diminished, and hope is brighter in my heart than once it was.

Watching Donny clamber across the split-rail fence and hurry south along the county road, as he races out of Hiskott's reach, I would like nothing more than to learn one day that he has taken the same journey of the heart that I have taken.

My sinuses weep, and my nose is a faucet. Much of the time, I find it difficult to sustain an image of myself as a man of action and a defender of the innocent.

Just as the mechanic disappears along the road, I smell smoke. The mayhem I have instigated must be evolving nicely. I need to reconnoiter.

By moving farther from the trees, I will be more easily seen, because my navy-blue sweatshirt and my jeans are in stark contrast to the sun-bleached grass around me. If someone spots me from afar I might not be recognized, but I don't dare take any chances.

Crouched low, with a .38 revolver in one hand and a

pistol in the other, I scuttle through the tall grass, alert for snakes because it seems to be that kind of day. As I press forward, insects spring into flight, leaves of grass and feathertop brushing against my face bring to mind the forked and tickling tongues of serpents, and I narrowly avoid stepping in a pile of deer poop.

The meadow begins to slope, and I come to a place where I can see the descending hills of Harmony Corner and the sea beyond. I lie down and raise my head just high enough to study the seven Victorian houses that stand a few hundred yards below, to the west and slightly farther south of my position. If any guards are stationed around the uppermost of those residences, where Dr. Hiskott makes his lair, they are well concealed.

Perhaps three hundred yards to the north lies the demolished big rig, the detached tractor on its side beneath the Monterey cypress. Both the tractor and the tree have caught fire, after all, and flames seethe up through the branches, which across decades have been sculpted by the wind into elegant southeast-leaning forms that are reminiscent of lines of Japanese calligraphy. Whatever the wind has written over time, fire rapidly erases and disperses as oily black smoke.

People have gone down into those hills, no doubt seeking the truck driver, but at this distance it's impossible to know which of them are members of the Harmony family, under

Hiskott's rule, and which are patrons of the diner. Nor am I able to get an accurate count of them. They are small figures at this remove.

The larger blaze is closer than the one consuming the cypress. The tumbling propane tank, fire gouting from the open valve, must have looked like a flamethrower in the grip of a furious poltergeist. The fire line in its wake follows a sinuous path, a leaping tossing brightness that, like an agitated dragon, wriggles down one slope and up another.

The intensity of this blaze is much greater than I anticipated. Evidently no wildfire has occurred here in a long time, and previous years of grass have died and been compacted into a dense dry sod that burns aggressively, so that it isn't the grass of a single year that fuels this tempest. The rising smoke from the conflagration is pale gray, almost white, billowing in alarming volume, rapidly forming high columns that, in this still air, seem to support the sky.

Although I am no more a pyromaniac than I am a brain surgeon, I can't help but take some satisfaction from the scene. Besides distracting Hiskott and his army of slaves, I need to generate at least some smoke at ground level to screen my approach to the target house. Most of the white masses churn straight up from the burning turf; however, a thin, lower haze creeps downhill. Soon I should have the conditions I require.

To an uninformed observer, my grin might appear to be

wicked. I congratulate myself aloud—"Fine work, bucko"—and wipe my dripping nose on a sleeve of my sweatshirt as though I am a filthy pirate preparing to plunder and destroy a seaside settlement. Sometimes, I wonder to what criminal depths I might descend if ever I went over to the dark side.

A tanker truck, half the size of an eighteen-wheeler, appears at the crest of the blacktop lane that connects the businesses to the houses below. On the white tank are two words in red—HARMONY CORNER—and I can only suppose that this is a loaded-and-ready piece of firefighting equipment, a wise precaution in a part of California where some rainy seasons produce only an occasional drizzle and where wildfires will periodically blacken the land.

From the houses, an extended-bed Dodge pickup appears, with six men from the Harmony clan seated in the cargo area. The truck is a beefed-up beauty, jacked high on large tires, and it's fitted with a V-shaped plow, currently raised. It stops on the blacktop halfway between the houses and the fire.

The guys in the back of the pickup, armed with shovels and hoes, bail out and marshal along the shoulder of the lane. The driver pulls off the pavement, lowers the big V-shaped blade, and drives into the field, plowing a firebreak toward the sea. At once the men follow the truck, hoeing away the loosened grass, spading up any chunks that the plow didn't churn loose, creating a six- or eight-foot width of bare earth.

With no wind to chase the fire, it might spread slowly enough for the truck to make a return pass from shore to road, establishing a twelve- or sixteen-foot barrier. In this stillness, the flames will not be able to jump across a swath that wide.

Farther up the lane, the tanker truck comes to a stop. The man hanging on the back of it drops off, and two women exit the cab. The three set to work in what appears to be a much-practiced plan, and I can imagine only that the truck has a powerful pump and fire hose that will direct a quenching stream of water deep into the grassland.

One of the problems of making it up as you go along—my modus operandi—is that sometimes you find yourself pitted against people who have a well-considered plan and are expert at executing it.

I counsel myself that although events have turned against me, there's always a chance they will tip once more in my favor.

Then I sneeze. The scent of Bermuda Guy's aftershave lingers in the sinuses as might a skunk's malodor, the dry grass in which I lie smells of dust and chaff, and although the ground-level smoke is too thin to offer concealment, it is acrid enough to burn like the fumes of a habanero pepper in my nostrils. Explosive sneezes reduce me to a parody of a red-eyed allergy sufferer in a TV commercial for an antihistamine. I'm sure I can't be heard at any significant distance, but I put down the guns and bury my face in my hands, muffling the sound, glad that these are essentially *dry* sneezes.

If I were Batman, my cape would already be on fire.

Suddenly, a breeze. The grass around me shivers and flutters toward the south and east. And the breeze grows stronger. They say a blaze in the wild can generate its own wind, but I think that has to be a big firestorm.

Surprised out of my sneezing for a moment, I see the invisible wind by its effects, as it angles through Harmony Corner from the northwest, off the sea and across the hilly meadows. The flames feed more voraciously on the grass and leap higher, and from the Monterey cypress, scabs of burning bark peel away and, airborne, carry the contagion of fire over the heads of those who fight it, infecting grass beyond them. The new smoke doesn't ascend vertically, instead rises at a shallow angle, and a soft tide rolls toward the tanker truck, toward the firebreak crew.

I am getting the chaos I wanted. The problem is, you can switch chaos on, but chaos itself is in control of the off switch.

Twenty

ED, ONCE CALLED ALADDIN, IS THE FIRST artificial intelligence I've ever known. Maybe if Harry can kill Hiskott and if then I live long enough to see the world become the total science-fiction theme park it seems to be headed toward, I'll probably know dozens of them one day. Let me tell you, if they're all as nice as Ed has turned out to be, that's okay with me.

So after he breaks the beastly news to me—that if the FBI ever knows where Dr. Hiskott went and what he's been doing these past five years and all, they'll quarantine my whole family forever—Ed asks me to sit at one of the workstations in the sphere-observation room. As I park my butt in the chair, the computer switches on even though I don't touch it.

Although the whole freaking government will throw my family in the slammer of all slammers, Ed says my Harry Potter, cute as he is, isn't the only one who can help us, that there is another. Well, as you can imagine, I have a need to know who that is.

"First things first," Ed says.

On the computer screen appears a head shot of Harry in the yellow hallway where Orc lies mummified.

"You have cameras everywhere, huh?"

"Not everywhere. But wherever there is a security camera or a computer with an online link and Skype capacity, or a cell phone with a camera function, anywhere in the world, I have eyes."

"Whoa. That's a whack upside the head. I guess with artificial intelligence, just like with natural intelligence, there can be a way-creepy side."

"Would you rather that I were blind, Jolie Ann Harmony?"

"Well, now I feel seriously mean. No, Ed, I don't wish you were blind. I just hope you never watch me in the bathroom or anything."

"Security cameras are not installed in bathrooms, and neither are computers with Skype capacity."

"Well, I guess that's mostly right."

"If you take a smartphone into the bathroom, I would advise you to keep it switched off."

"For sure."

"I guarantee you, Jolie Ann Harmony, that I personally have no interest in watching human beings in bathrooms."

"I didn't really think you did, Ed. I'm sorry if I seemed to imply you were a pervert or something. What I was thinking was, some other artificial intelligence someday might not be as respectful as you are."

"That is something to consider. I cannot vouch for the stability of any future artificial intelligences."

On the computer monitor, the photo of my Harry in the yellow hallway is replaced by a different photo of him that looks like it might have been in a newspaper.

Ed says, "Harry's real name is Odd Thomas."

"Odd?"

"Apparently, the origin of the name is a long story. We have no time for it now."

"How'd you learn his name?"

"I applied facial-recognition software to all the photos in the files of the California DMV but could not find him there."

"That's like millions of pictures. How long did *that* take?"

"Seven minutes. Thereafter, I searched the digitalized photo archives of the Associated Press."

The photo goes away and some video plays, a TV news story from like eighteen months earlier, about a terrible shooting in a shopping mall in Pico Mundo, forty-one wounded and nineteen dead. A policeman says there would have been many more dead except for the action of one brave young man, who happens to be Harry. I mean, Odd Thomas. The policeman says hundreds would have died if Odd hadn't taken down both gunmen and dealt with a truck full of explosives and all. The reporter says Odd won't talk to the press, he tells us that Odd says he didn't do anything special. Odd says anyone would have done what he did. The reporter says Odd is as shy as he is courageous, but even though I'm a kid and all, I know the right word isn't *shy*.

Earlier, you might remember, I explained how I loved him because he seemed brave and kind and sweet, also because there was something else about him, something different. And here it is. I *knew* that he wouldn't abandon us. I *knew* he wouldn't just run and save himself.

Ed says, "I show you this, Jolie Ann Harmony, because in spite of all your brave and wise-ass talk, in spite of the fact that I did not detect pheromones associated with lying, I did detect pheromones associated with despair. I have developed an affection for you, and thus it pains me to know that you are on the verge of losing hope."

"Not anymore," I tell him.

Over the years, when Hiskott has entered me to live through me, there's one thing I refuse to let him know:

what it feels like when I cry. My tears are mine, not his, never his. I'll save them forever rather than let the sick creep feel them hot on my cheeks or taste them at the corners of my mouth. If you really truly want to know, I've thought if I was ever free someday, I might discover I've held my tears so long that I can't cry anymore, that I'm a dry stone and nothing can ever be wrung from me. Yet now my vision blurs, and there are tears, tears of hope and happiness, although nothing's yet been won.

After a while, I remember: "Hey, Ed, you said there's someone else besides Harry . . . besides Odd. Someone who can help us."

"Yes, Jolie Ann Harmony. That would be me."

Twenty-one

IN THE JEEP GRAND CHEROKEE ONCE MORE, I am no longer sneezing. Perhaps Bermuda Guy's preferred aftershave and the grass-fire fumes happen to be two molecules that are like puzzle pieces and, locking together, neutralize each other. More likely, now that the time has come to take the plunge into Hiskott's lair, I so dread the upcoming encounter that I don't have the capacity to be annoyed by any scent or smoke. I once read that condemned men standing before firing squads, in the thrall of terror, have been observed to be oblivious of bees crawling on their faces even when the bees have stung them. One guy evidently mistook a bee sting for the killing shot and dropped dead on the spot, sparing his executioners the expense of ammunition.

Because I rarely forget anything, my brain is so packed with useless information that it constantly makes connections between bits of data that are at best tenuously linked. Sometimes I wonder if, at some critical moment, being distracted by thoughts about bee-stung condemned men will get me killed. But if you can't trust your own brain, what can you trust?

I shut off the air circulation in the Jeep to keep out as much smoke as possible, and I pilot the vehicle out of the trees, heading south across the high meadow. Visibility is down to sixty or seventy feet, except when small shifts in the direction of the breeze cause clean currents of air to open narrow lines of sight to farther points of Harmony Corner, but these close up as suddenly as they open.

Although I need the cover of smoke, this murk is thicker than I expected, forcing me to proceed slower than I would prefer—and *much* slower than I will need to drive a few minutes from now. Visibility rapidly declines to forty or fifty feet, and if it gets much worse, I might as well steer with my eyes closed.

Because I can't see any landmarks and because the Jeep odometer doesn't click off units of distance as short as three hundred feet, I rely on intuition when I turn the vehicle hard right and brake to a stop. I *think* I'm facing directly west, and I *think* the cluster of houses far below is slightly north of my position, so that I might be able to come in behind them.

The difference between what I think to be true and what *is* true, however, could lead to disaster. The hills below offer mostly gentle slopes, but there are a few steep drop-offs. If I mistakenly drive over one, the Grand Cherokee will at least tip into a catastrophic roll. In spite of the fact that the vehicle has four-wheel drive, if it lands on its side or roof, it'll be as useless as an airplane without wings.

Under this white-gray pall, the day is darker than it would be in an equally thick fog, because sunshine doesn't refract through smoke a fraction as well as it does through mist. Instead of light finding its way obliquely into Harmony Corner, much of it bounces off the soot suspended in the gaseous plumes, bringing an early dusk upon these acres. In this gloom that creeps steadily toward darkness, in this disorder that thwarts the senses, the amorphous smoky masses surging around the Grand Cherokee seem to be figures, many human and others fantastic, legions of harried spirits on some unholy pilgrimage.

I try the headlights, but the beams bounce off the swarming masses, reducing visibility from thirty feet to ten. The fog lights are likewise useless. And in the darkening murk, I could swear that faces form out of the graying smoke to sneer and snarl at me before dissolving in the passing.

If I am to find my way to Norris Hiskott, I will have to resort to psychic magnetism, which I trust won't lead me to a cliff. I don't know what he looks like, but I have his name, and I can picture the house he's claimed as his. Concentrating on that name and summoning that image into my mind's eye, trusting in impulse and intuition, I get ready to ease up on the brake pedal and drift forward wherever my peculiar power leads me.

What happens next is not easily described. A cold draft but not a real one, the mental equivalent of a draft, the *idea* of a draft, blows through my mind, as if a window has opened. Perhaps because I have been picturing the Victorian residence, I in fact see a window with sullen yellow light beyond and, in the light, a sleek silhouette that leaps toward the sill and the raised sash, eager to spring in upon me. Realizing that I have drawn to me the enemy that I hoped to be drawn *toward*, I slam the sash, at once turning my thoughts from Hiskott's name to Stormy Llewellyn's, instantly driving out the conjured image of the house with a memory of Stormy's face, because only she can fill my mind so completely that, in the moment of this assault, the puppeteer cannot find an entry point.

Even though I repelled Hiskott, though he did not for a second see through my eyes to obtain a solitary clue as to my position or intent, I continue to hold Stormy in mind, because the memory of her and the promise of the card from the fortune-telling machine—YOU ARE DESTINED TO BE TOGETHER FOREVER—constitute my best defense against discouragement, as well, and against fear.

In this situation, psychic magnetism is too dangerous to employ. Denied my special gift, I am left only with my wits, which is like Robin Hood having to trade his quiver of expertly crafted arrows for a couple of rocks.

Just then, Jolie Harmony speaks to me: "Are you there, Harry Potter? This is Jolie. Are you there?"

Surprised and mystified, I am for just a moment reduced to the superstition of a remote-island primitive who, ignorant of the marvels of modern technology, can conclude only that, by the use of magic, a shaman has reduced Jolie to the size of my thumb and has transported her into the radio of the Grand Cherokee.

"Are you there, Harry?" she asks again.

"Jolie? Where—"

"Well, see, those steel doors I couldn't pry open just opened by themselves after you left, and so now I'm in this mega-weird place in Fort Wyvern, called Project Polaris. This is where old Doc Hiskott worked, there's this alien artifact and all, and he was dissecting dead ETs for some stupid reason, which is when everything went to hell. The doc got mixed up with alien DNA, he's like some hybrid now. He was nuts to begin with—all right, not psychotic but a neurotic freak. He strangled his wife and all, we don't know was it because of nagging or because he had no fingernails. But there aren't any people here anymore, because of the mothballs, so there's just me and Ed."

I manage to get out, "How are you able to—"

And Jolie sails on: "What Ed is able to do, he's able to slip into just about any wired or wireless communications thing and use it without anyone knowing. So since you're in a Jeep Grand Cherokee, vanity license-plate number COOL DUDE, that happens to be equipped with OnStar, Ed could locate you by GPS. We know exactly where you are, and I'm talking to you by way of their satellite-communications system. Pretty wow, huh?"

"But how could you know—"

"See, Ed can do like sixteen things at once. So one thing he did even while he was telling me who you really were, he checked for any 911 calls to the sheriff from customers at the Corner that might tell us are you stirring things up already. Jumpin' jackrabbits, you don't waste time! Some guy phones in his truck is stolen, some other guy phones in the truck goes flying—"

I'm not sure which is the most disorienting: the blinding smoke churning around the Grand Cherokee and all the world lost in it, or the foul air from the wildfire that's making me a little dizzy, or Jolie's excited chatter.

"—some other guy phones in his Grand Cherokee is stolen, and some *other* guy phones in a grass fire. So Ed is learning all this neat stuff while he's showing me who you are, and then in like seven seconds he finds out the Jeep has OnStar. So here we are, and we want to help."

I clear my throat and ask, "Who's Ed?"

"Shoot, that's right," Jolie says, "you couldn't know. Ed is a computer. No, wait, that's an insult, I guess. Ed's not just a silly computer, he's an artificial intelligence, another big secret project here at Wyvern. He doesn't want to take over the world and all, of course he doesn't, he's made that perfectly clear to everyone. So when they mothballed this Project Polaris, they put Ed in charge of watching over it, keeping it all safe. You'll like Ed, he's fun, he can do like twenty things at the same time."

"I thought you said sixteen."

"Heck, Ed's so smart he can probably do twenty *times* twenty things simultaneously. Say hello, Ed."

A low, mellow, yet slightly ominous voice says, "It is an honor to make your acquaintance, Odd Thomas."

Jolie says, "Oh, yeah, that's another thing, Harry. I know you're not Harry Potter. I mean, I've always known you weren't Harry Potter, he isn't real. But now I know who you really are, and you're what I knew you would be, a hero who says he's not a hero. I knew you would come to us one day, I always knew, but I didn't know your name would be Odd Thomas. Now you're here, and everything's going to be all right."

"Things are still a long way from being all right, Jolie."

Although all the vents are closed and the fans are turned off, the air in the Cherokee grows dirtier by the minute.

I ask, "Ed, are you there?"

"Yes, Odd Thomas, I am here. How may I assist you?"

I decide to accept everything that Jolie tells me, because the whole story sounds too crazy to be anything but the truth.

My unusual life has taught me that the world is profoundly more complex and far stranger than most people are able—or willing—to recognize. What most people call truth is merely the surface, and under it lies a great depth of truth that they do not perceive. A large part of my time is spent coping with the spirits of the lingering dead, poltergeists, eerie creatures that I call bodachs, prophetic dreams, and all kinds of one-off moments of supernatural weirdness, as well as with horrendous human miscreants of every imaginable variety; consequently, it strikes me as refreshing, almost prosaic, to be caught up in a supernatural-free incident involving top-secret government projects, an artificial intelligence that does not want to rule the world, half-breed extraterrestrials, and the women who love—and are strangled by—them.

"Ed, is Jolie really safe where she is now?"

"Safer than she has been for many years. No harm will come to Jolie Ann Harmony in my domain."

"If any harm does come to her in your domain, I'll find your plug and pull it."

"You don't have to threaten Ed," Jolie assures me. "There's not a bad circuit in the guy, and that's certified once every hour by a self-analysis program. Anyway, he can't lie."

"You really can't lie, Ed?"

"My creators programmed me so that should I ever speak a single untruth, I will immediately identify what I have done by singing 'Liar, liar, pants on fire.' "

"Which is kind of funny," Jolie says, "because he doesn't even wear pants."

Still wary, I press Ed: "Why couldn't a self-aware artificial intelligence evolve to the point where it could override parts of its basic program?"

After a silence, Ed replies: "Why cannot a bright and gifted young man of almost twenty-two ever quite get over the psychological pain inflicted on him so many years ago by his mentally unbalanced mother?"

Now it's my turn to be silent.

And then there's only one possible reply. "I'm sorry that I threatened to unplug you, Ed."

"You did so with only the best of motives, Odd Thomas. Your concern for Jolie Ann Harmony is admirable, and in fact I share it."

"How did you know . . . about my mother?"

"After events in Pico Mundo, there were some mentions in the media about your family, certain speculations."

"I never read any of that."

Instead of rushing past the windows, the smoke is for a moment caught in a vortex of hot air and swirls around the Grand Cherokee. I feel as if the vehicle is being levitated and spun, as it might be in a tornado, and I close my eyes.

"Ed, was it you who opened that sealed drain, so I didn't have to go back by way of the beach?"

"Yes."

"Thank you."

"You are welcome, Odd Thomas."

"When you led me that way, did you know I'd hijack a truck?"

"I was not surprised when you did."

"But I didn't know I was going to do it until I climbed out of that manhole and found myself outside Harmony Corner. I made it up as I went along. So how did you know?"

"A consideration of all possibilities and an analysis of the viability of each suggested that hijacking a truck and doing what you did with it was the option most likely to help you achieve your goal. My observation of you, in your discussions with Jolie Ann Harmony, suggested to me that, in spite of your self-deprecating manner, you usually make the correct decisions in such matters."

Jolie interprets: "I think what Ed means is you kick butt."

Ed has a question: "Now tell me, Odd Thomas, did you take Purvis Eugene Beamer's smartphone?"

"What? I don't know any Purvis Beamer."

"You are driving the vehicle that he reported stolen."

"Oh. Bermuda Guy. No, I didn't take his smartphone."

"Two GPS-reporting signals related to Purvis Eugene Beamer are being emitted from the same map coordinates."

When I open my eyes, the smoke is no longer swirling around the Jeep, merely surging past as before.

"Yeah. I see it now. His phone's in one of the cup holders."

"Take it and put it in a pocket. Then we will be able to remain in contact even when you have gravely damaged that vehicle."

"How do you know I'm going to gravely damage it?"

"I have deduced your intentions, Odd Thomas."

Jolie says, "He's like super-smart, Oddie. In a kind of way, he was homeschooled like me, in a lab instead of a home, by scientists instead of by his mom, since he doesn't have a real mom. But he's humongously smarter, not because he studies harder than I do, but because he can absorb entire ginormous libraries in minutes, and because he's never bored with anything like I am. It's kind of sad he doesn't have a mom and all. Don't you think it's sad? It's not so sad you want to lie around all day sobbing through a thousand Kleenex, but sad enough."

Twenty-two

ED WILL BE MY NATTY BUMPPO, THE UNLIKELY
name of the scout in *The Last of the Mohicans*, who was
also known as Hawkeye. From his electronic aerie, he will
show me the way through the blinding drifts of smoke.

The Jeep Grand Cherokee with the COOL DUDE
license plate is equipped not just with OnStar's real-time
voice communication, but also with GPS navigation. GPS
maps include all streets, county roads, state routes, and
federal highways, but if you decide to go off-road, you're
on your own; the graphics on the monitor won't be able
to warn you about treacherous features of the open land,
and the recorded, guiding voice of that businesslike yet
somewhat sultry lady who provides direction will fall
silent in disapproval.

Fortunately, Ed enjoys instant access to the latest digitized surveys of the planet conducted by satellite, and therefore he knows the most minute details of the terrain in Harmony Corner, as well as in just about anywhere else you can name. He is able precisely to locate the Jeep Grand Cherokee by the identifying signal that its transponder continuously broadcasts. His voice has not a scintilla of sultriness, but I am calmed and made confident by his assurances that he can assist me in achieving my goal, which the density of the smoke has seemed to put beyond my reach.

"In the first phase of the approach," Ed says, "drive slowly. Will you drive slowly, Odd Thomas?"

"Yes. Yes, I will, Ed."

"You must listen closely to my instructions and follow them to the letter."

"Of course. Yes."

"If I were to tell you to turn the steering wheel a quarter of a revolution to the left and you turned it forty percent—"

"I would never do that."

"—you might drive directly into a sinkhole that we are trying to avoid. Another thing, Odd Thomas—do not interrupt me."

"I won't, Ed."

"You just did."

"I won't do it again."

"I am not a harsh taskmaster and certainly not a tyrant."

"I didn't think you were, Ed."

Jolie says, "He really doesn't want to rule the world."

"However," Ed says, "if this is going to work, I must give you precise instructions, and you must follow them precisely."

"I understand."

"In my experience," Ed says, "human beings frequently say that they understand, when in fact they do not understand at all."

"But I *do* understand. You'll just have to trust me, Ed."

"I suppose I must. However, if through no fault of mine, you drive over a cliff to your death, I will be sad."

"If I do, I won't blame you, Ed."

"That will be insufficient consolation."

The girl says, "You won't drive over a cliff—will you, Oddie?"

"No, Jolie, I won't. Though I might bash my head on the steering wheel until my brains come out my ears, if we don't get started *now*."

Ed is baffled. "Why would you bash your head on the steering wheel, Odd Thomas?"

"It's just an expression of frustration, Ed. I didn't mean it."

"If you would bash your brains out, there is no point in our going forward with this plan."

"I would never do such a thing, Ed. I swear."

"I do not detect any vocal patterns of deceit."

"Because I'm telling the truth, Ed. May we begin?"

"Drive directly forward at five miles an hour."

Following the foregoing reminder that life often is as shot through with absurdity as it is with terror and joy, phase one of the approach to Hiskott begins.

For all that I can see, the whole world might be smouldering, its entire substance being steadily converted to gasses and soot. Maybe the smoke is less white and more gray than before, or maybe the layer of crud gathered over the Corner is so thick now that, short of going nova, the sun can't penetrate it.

In spite of the smell of burning grass, the fumes that sting my eyes, and the hot irritation in my throat, the realm through which I travel seems to be a steadily darkening sea full of stirred silt and clouds of minute plankton. As I follow Ed's directions down the hills, I feel as though I am descending into an oceanic abyss where eventually I will find myself in perfect blackness eons old, where eyeless and pressure-deformed creatures eke out a desperate living in a dark cold desolation.

I suspect that this feeling of sinking ever deeper has less to do with the formless, surging masses beyond the windows of the Jeep than with the fact that I am drawing nearer to the thing that once was Norris Hiskott. It's now a unique entity of singular malevolence, and the pressure that I sense isn't pressure at all, but instead the black-hole gravity of its evil.

Although every vent in the vehicle is tightly shut, the air seems to be increasingly polluted, and a variety of claustrophobia overcomes me, a sense of being trapped in a place where I will slowly suffocate. I sneeze once, twice, a third time.

"Gesundheit."

"Thank you, Ed."

Shortly after that exchange, he tells me to brake to a stop and informs me that I have arrived at the brink of the slope that leads down to the backyard of the residence in which Hiskott has spent the past five years becoming . . . whatever he has become. Although the murk surrounding the Jeep seems fractionally less oppressive than before, I can see nothing of the house.

Ed agrees that my original strategy and tactics are the most likely to succeed. Because he's able to consult Google Earth for a look-down on the building, he can refine my approach enough to substantially increase my chances of success.

At his suggestion, I release my safety harness long enough to pick up the pistol and the revolver from the passenger seat. I tuck them under my belt, the pistol against my abdomen, the revolver in the small of my back.

I buckle up once more and lean forward, both hands on the wheel.

Monitoring the GPS transponders on various county fire-control-agency vehicles, Ed suggests that I wait another forty seconds until those trucks are about to enter Harmony Corner. Their sirens will add to the cacophony and further mask the noise I will be making. He says that sheriff's deputies are close behind.

Generally speaking, these harrowing moments in my unusual life, when I am compelled to reckless action and violence, do not thrill me, do not have any quality of positive excitement or exhilaration. They are characterized by fear that must not be allowed to ripen into incapacitating terror, by abhorrence, by consternation that is mostly an expectation of the confusion that usually arises in the thick of action, the battleground confusion that can be the death of me.

This, however, is one of those rare occasions in which I'm also exhilarated. I feel so *right* about the commitment of life and limb that I anticipate the pending encounter with exuberance. I might not be capable of the offhand amusement and ready quips of James Bond, but I do feel that taking it to the bad guys can be at times a lively and beguiling sport.

Over the years, I have noticed that these special moments are always in situations where I'm not struggling alone against some mortal threat, when I have the support of people whom I like and trust. Loyal companions are an unequaled grace, staunching fear before it bleeds you numb, a reliable antidote for creeping despair. This is true even when my team is comprised of a twelve-year-old girl a mile or more removed from the action and an artificial intelligence who has no body that might be shot or bludgeoned, or torn, as I might be shot, bludgeoned, and torn.

But, hey, I prefer our tomboy Jolie to Batman's Robin in those embarrassing girly tights of his, and our Ed goes a long way toward rehabilitating the image of artificial intelligences that HAL 9000 ruined more than four decades earlier.

"Fire trucks arriving," Ed alerts me. "Sirens loud, cover good, time to go."

En route, he's told me what I must do. Hold the wheel straight, drift neither left nor right. Don't deviate from a direct downhill course to the house. The land is hard-packed from much sun and little rain, and supposedly it has no significant irregularities that might jolt me off course. Even Ed, with all his resources for data and his powers of computation, can't calculate the precise speed at which I should arrive at my destination, although he advises that anything under forty miles per hour might be inadequate and anything over sixty is likely to leave me incapacitated.

When he says *go*, I accelerate rapidly into the blinding miasma, which races across the windshield like clouds might rush across the cockpit windows of an aircraft. Ed says the slope is long, giving me all the territory I require to build speed. The tall, dry grass, not yet on fire here, rustles under the Cherokee and swishes against its flanks, so that it sounds as if I'm racing through a shallow stream. Tires stutter on summer-baked earth that rain has not yet softened, but they have good traction. Although vibrations travel through the frame into the steering wheel, I have no trouble maintaining control.

Suddenly the false dusk relents, sunlight swells through the diminishing billows of soot and ash, and as I achieve fifty miles per hour, I am no longer blind. Here, nearer the shore, the stiff breeze angling in from the northwest pushes the smoke farther inland, leaving this most remote corner of the Corner draped only in a blue haze.

As Ed ascertained by reviewing aerial shots of the property on Google Earth, the target house, which has a large front porch, offers no porch here in back, only a patio with a trellis cover on which nothing grows. A single door most likely opens to the kitchen, and a pair of large French sliding doors probably serve the family room, which in the absence of a family is now used for God knows what purpose by the half-human Hiskott. The outdoor furniture and potted plants that might once have made a pleasant space of the patio have long previously been taken away, and nothing stands between me and those French sliders.

Because my existence is greatly complicated by my paranormal abilities, I strive always to keep the rest of my life simple, which is why I work as a fry cook, when I work at all, and which is why, when rarely I daydream of a career change, I consider only a job in shoe sales or maybe tire sales, which seems undemanding. I have few material possessions, no retirement account, and I do not own—and never have owned—a car. What I am about to do to Purvis Beamer's Jeep Grand Cherokee is confirmation enough that, even if I had the money to purchase a nice car, I would be unwise to do so, because with a vehicle of my own to sacrifice in an emergency like this, I would never steal that of another.

I'm safely harnessed. I trust—as I must—the impact-reduction technology in contemporary vehicles, which involves the absorption of energy through the tactical and engineered collapse of certain parts of their structure. Nevertheless, approaching the patio, I slide down in the driver's seat as far as the harness will allow, to minimize the chance that I will be decapitated by something that might slam through the windshield. As the tires find the patio, I let go of the steering wheel and cover my face with my hands, as a child might do at the brink of the first big drop in a roller-coaster track.

An instant before impact, I move my right foot from accelerator to brake pedal. The crash must be loud, but it doesn't seem so to me, because the air bag deploys, briefly enveloping me as though it is a gigantic prophylactic, muffling the sound of the collision. At the moment when the bag warmly embraces me, I jam my foot down on the brake, the wood of the French sliders cracks like a quick volley of rifle shots, tortured metal shrieks, and the windshield shatters. Fishtailing into the room, the Grand Cherokee batters through what I imagine to be sofas and chairs and other furniture, although I am not foolish enough even to *hope* that the Hiskott thing has just been killed while napping in a La-Z-Boy.

As the air bag deflates and as the Grand Cherokee comes to a stop, I switch off the engine. If the fuel tank has been ruptured, I want to avoid igniting a blaze that might draw the attention of the county firefighters away from the grass fire farther north in Harmony Corner.

I appear to be uninjured. In the morning, I'll probably suffer from whiplash and other pains, but now everything seems to work.

The driver's door is buckled, won't open. The passenger door still functions. As I get out of the vehicle, I draw the pistol from under my sweatshirt, reminding myself that the magazine contains only seven rounds, not ten.

The wreckage in the family room makes it difficult to

know quite what the place must have been like before I arrived. But there are cobwebs in the corners of the ceiling, a mobile of moths and flies in one of them, suggesting that the spider never lived to taste the prey that was enchanted by its architecture, and everywhere is a layer of dust that couldn't have settled over everything in this first minute after the Jeep broke the doors down.

Pistol in a two-hand grip, I sweep the room left to right. No one. Nothing.

North of here, the sirens of the fire trucks groan into silence. The only sounds in the house are the ticks and creaks of the tortured Grand Cherokee cooling down, settling into ruin.

Hiskott might have expected me to attempt a break-in, but of a more conventional kind. He won't have anticipated this. But he surely knows I'm here now, and my success depends on moving quickly, before one of the family, possessed, shows up in a killing frenzy.

A glance at the windows reveals that although the air is largely clear around this house and its neighbors on the flat ground below, the rest of Harmony Corner remains socked in by churning clouds of soot and ash. The marker lights and the warning lights of the fire trucks pulse and swivel deep within that seething murk, flinging off red-and-blue apparitions that chase one another through the scudding smoke.

An archway connects the family room to a large eat-in kitchen with an island. Crumbs, stale crusts of bread, desiccated cheese rinds, dried spills of sauces, and moldering wads of unidentifiable food litter the countertops. Scores of ants crawl through the debris, but they don't scurry busily in efficient lines of march as do most ordinary ants; instead, they wander desultorily across the counters, as though they have consumed a toxin that leaves them confused and without purpose.

Piles of bones litter the filthy floor. Ham bones, beef bones, chicken bones, and others. Some have been broken as if to facilitate access to the marrow.

One of the pair of cabinet doors under the double sink has been torn off its hinges and is nowhere to be seen. From the space beyond spills a brittle drift of what appear to be dozens of rat skulls and skeletons, each sucked as clean as a turkey drumstick provided to a starving man. Not a scrap of skin or fur remains on any of them, and not a single length of scaly tail has been discarded.

The cooktop is encrusted with charred food and filth, less like a stove than like the unholy altar of some primitive temple with a long, cruel history of grisly sacrifices. I doubt that the propane-fired burners have worked in two or three years. The assumption has to be made that everything Dr. Hiskott consumes has, for a long time, been eaten raw.

According to Jolie and her mother, Ardys, the family brings their ruler everything he demands, including a great deal of food, which I believe they leave just inside the front door. I doubt that they brought him the rats.

I have been expecting a hybrid of a man and an extraterrestrial that will be far advanced beyond the condition of a human being, as clear-eyed and formidable as it also might be strange beyond easy comprehension. This unsettling evidence seems to argue instead for devolution: if not a steep intellectual decline, at least a severe diminishment of Hiskott's ability to hold fast to any cultural norms and to repress animal compulsions.

A pantry door stands ajar, darkness beyond. Pistol still in a two-hand grip, I toe the door open wide. The inspill of pale light reveals that the shelves are bare. Not one can of vegetables or jar of fruit, or box of pasta. Sitting on the floor is a headless human skeleton. The skull rests on a shelf separate from the other bones, and a detached arm lies on the floor, one finger extended, pointed toward me as if I am expected. Neither the bones nor the floor under them are marked by the stains of decomposing flesh.

This discovery necessitates a correction to the Harmony-family history of the past five years. The skeleton is that of a child, perhaps a boy of about eight. If members of the family buried Maxy in an unmarked grave in some far corner of their property, then either the Hiskott thing ventured forth that very night to retrieve the corpse for his larder—or the dead boy was left with him, and Hiskott fashioned for the family false memories of an interment. This final twist to the story of Maxy's already-horrific death is so unthinkable that, should I live, it will be my obligation to keep it from them. Neither Jolie nor anyone close to her must know, at least not until many years of freedom and peace have faded this part of their past as if it were a fever dream.

In this house of secrets, I feel displaced in time and space, as if, by the power of the alien presence, this land exists more on the planet of the creature's origin than here on Earth, as if I live now not less than two years after losing Stormy but dwell instead in the dark future, on the eve of the end-of-all event that will explain the history of the universe.

The downstairs hallway is like a tunnel to the afterlife in a film about near-death experiences, a shadowy length that telescopes toward a mysterious light, though the promise at the farther end is not bright or inviting, but pallid, wintry, and uncertain. A switch turns on three ceiling fixtures. The bulbs are burned out in the second and third of them.

In the fall of light, immediately to my right, a door stands open on a landing, beyond which stairs lead down into an unrelenting darkness. A stench rises from what lies below, a witches' brew of rancid fat, rotten vegetation, urine, and other foulness unknown. Something moves in that deep dankness, what might be heavy horn-heeled feet knocking and scraping along a concrete floor, and a voice issues an eerie trilling sound.

I try the switch on the landing wall, but it doesn't summon any light. I pull the door shut. There is a deadbolt, which I engage. If eventually I must go into the cellar, I will require a flashlight. Before that, I need to clear the rooms on the first two floors, and hope to survive that inspection.

I move through a dining room long unused, revealed in sunlight filtered by gauzy curtains that hang between open draperies, through a study where bevies of fat moths quail from the window sheers and flutter to darker corners as if the shadows will save them from me, and then I return to the hallway, proceeding toward the foyer and the front rooms.

I am no less afraid, but my fear is tempered now by a healthy detestation and by a conviction that my mission is something even more important than freeing the Harmony family from this curse. In some fundamental sense, I am here to perform an exorcism.

Twenty-three

SO HERE WE ARE, INSIDE WYVERN, AND MIGHT as well be a thousand miles away from Oddie for all the help we can give him. We hear him crash into the house as planned, but right after that we lose contact with him, because the car is probably smashed up and all. Ed says the Jeep is still transmitting a signal, and so is the smartphone. He's sure that Odd is alive and well. Okay, so Ed's super-smart, but that doesn't mean he knows everything, he's not like God or anything. As you can imagine, I want him to call that phone and see if Oddie's all right, but Ed says not yet, give Oddie time to orient himself, we don't want to distract him at a critical moment.

One of our three big worries, if we can limit them to three, is that when Oddie rocketed into the house, the boom of it alerted the county firefighting crew, and that they'll rush to the house, see what Hiskott cannot afford for them to see, and lots of people will die before it's over. But Ed is monitoring the emergency-band radio traffic plus all phone and cell-phone calls from anywhere in the Corner, and he says nobody seems to have noticed. The sirens, wind, fire, and just general commotion must have provided enough cover for Oddie.

I'm half sick thinking about it, but one of our other biggest worries is that Hiskott will use someone in my family to kill Oddie or that Oddie will have to kill some people in my family when he's attacked. Either way, you know, it's like I might just die myself if that happens, or if I don't die, then something in me will die, and I won't ever be the same or want to be.

If you want to know, the third thing that's making us nuts—or making me nuts, since Ed just isn't capable of being made nuts—is thinking about those three guests of the motor court that Hiskott took into his house over the years, those loners nobody missed, and they never came out again. Ed thinks maybe crazy old Hiskott might have done something more than mind-control them. He says maybe, after that injection of alien cells and over time, Hiskott is more alien now than human, and so he was able to infect those three and turn them into something alien, too. You know, like with a vampire bite or something less stupid than a vampire bite. Ed knows everything Hiskott and his team learned about the ETs, because he has access to those files. He says it's major scarifying stuff. So whatever Oddie's got to deal with in that house, it's not a close encounter of the third kind in the cuddly Spielberg style.

Over the past five years, I've said my best prayers every night, haven't missed a night, though I gotta admit, if it wouldn't break my mother's heart, I'd probably have stopped a year ago. I mean, praying to be free of Hiskott only makes me expect to be free *soon*, and then when the prayer's never answered, you feel even worse, and you wonder what's the point. I'm not criticizing God, if that's what you think, because nobody knows why God does things or how He thinks, and He's humongously smarter than any of us, even smarter than Ed. They say He works in *mysterious ways*, which is for sure true. What I'm saying is, maybe the whole praying business is a human idea, maybe God never asked us to do it. Yeah, all right, He wants us to like Him, and He wants us to respect Him, so we'll live right and do good. But God is good—right?—and to be really good you've got to have humility, we all know that, so then if God is the best of the best, then He's also the humblest of the humble. Right? So maybe it embarrasses Him to be praised like around the clock, to be called great and mighty all the time. And maybe it makes Him a little bit nuts the way we're always asking Him to solve our problems instead of even trying to solve them ourselves, which He made us so we could do. Anyway, so after almost giving up on prayer, and being pretty darned sure that God is too humble to sit around all day listening to us praise Him and beg Him, the funny thing is, I'm praying like crazy for Oddie. I guess I'm hopeless.

Twenty-four

AS I REACH THE END OF THE DOWNSTAIRS hall, from behind me comes the sound of the knob rattling in the cellar door. The door is a good mahogany slab, the deadbolt thick, the hinges blackened iron. Great effort will be needed to break it down, and the noise will give me plenty of warning. The rattling stops and all is quiet.

The six-pane sidelights flanking the front door admit only a dim and wintry light into the foyer, partly because acid-etched patterns of ivy vines frost significant areas of the glass. Also, the front porch faces west, away from the fullest brightness of the morning sun. The windowsills are gray with thick dust, littered with dead gnats, dead flies, dead spiders.

To the left, a living room is overfurnished with

floral-pattern chesterfields laden with decorative pillows, handsome wing chairs with footstools, curio cabinets, and several plant stands in which once-flourishing ferns now hang in brown sprays of parched fronds, the carpet under them littered with dead pinnules. Everywhere there is dust, cobwebs, stillness, and the air seems more humid toward the front of the house than in the back.

To the right of the foyer, a mahogany-paneled library offers an impressive collection of books, but they emit the odor of mildew. When I switch on the lights, a multitude of moths shiver out of the bookshelves, abandoning their feast of damp dust jacket and rotten binding cloth, by far more of them here than in the study. They swoop this way and that for a moment, agitated but without purpose.

A few take refuge on the ceiling, others settle upon a pair of club chairs upholstered in a shade of brown leather with which they blend, and the mass of them swarm toward me, past me, out of the room. Their soft bodies and softer wings flutter against my face, which I turn down and away from them, chilled by the contact to a degree that surprises me.

In the center of the library stands an antique pool table with elaborately carved legs and two carved and gilded lions as the cross supports that connect the legs. Silverfish skitter across the green-felt playing surface, disappearing into the ball pockets.

Even in the most disturbing environments, in the presence of deeply corrupt people who want nothing less than to kill me, I tend to find a vein of fun in either the rock or the hard place between which I'm trapped. Not this time. The atmosphere in this house is pestilential, poisonous, so unwholesome that I feel as if the most dangerous thing I've ever done is breathe the air herein.

At one end of the pool table lies an object that is no less enigmatical upon close inspection than from a distance. Round but not perfectly so, about five feet in diameter, it resembles nothing so much as a giant version of the medicine ball that men used to throw to one another for exercise before health clubs became high-tech. The object is mottled several shades of gray and is grained like leather, but it has no seams or stitching, and the lacquered sheen is unlike any leather finish I have ever seen. Some of the bulbs are burned out in the chandelier above the pool table, but what light there is glimmers in the surface of this unfathomable construction much the way that moonlight plays on dark water.

My perception of the object's nature changes from one instant to the next when the surface proves to be not lacquered but wet. A bead of moisture swells out of it and trickles down the curved form to the carpet. Then something within the great ball writhes.

As I back hurriedly away, the surface of the thing is

revealed to be rather like a cloak but not of cloth, of skin, which now peels up with a slick slithering sound, revealing a crouched form that in this unveiling rises with alarming alacrity to a height of almost seven feet. The limbs are jointed in ways that suggest machinery rather than bone, but this is no robot. It seems both reptilian and insectile, its flesh so tightly strung on its legs and arms that it appears withered but nonetheless strong. In the torso, in the set of the shoulders, it seems less reptilian and less insectile than human, and of course it stands erect. The gray cloaklike mass of skin falls in folds around it, less like a coat than like a cape, and its flesh is otherwise pale with muddy-yellow striations.

I would run, but I know that to turn my back will be to invite attack. Besides, everything about it speaks of speed, and it will have me before I've gone a dozen steps.

Because of my disturbed mother and her resort to threats with firearms as a primary child-raising technique, I have all my life disliked guns, though at this moment I *love* the one in my hands. I hesitate to use it only because I don't yet know the full nature of my adversary, for its face remains concealed in the dark cowl that is part of its cape-like garment of loose skin.

The creature lifts its hung head, the cowl peels away to settle around its neck like a rolled collar, and the face appears more human than not. Female. Greasy coils of dark hair. Features that might have been lovely before the skull elongated and the bones thickened during whatever transformation she endured at Hiskott's hand.

Here is one of the motor-court guests who was so alone in the world that she would not be missed, now a human-alien hybrid that perhaps exists for no reason but to protect and serve her master. If any of her former personality remains, any slightest degree of self-awareness and memory, what a horror her current existence must be, and how insane that kernel of her true self must have become in this monstrous prison of strange flesh and bone.

Although the beast's eyes are milky as if with cataracts, I am sure that it can see, perhaps as well in the dark as in the light. I can't look away from those eyes, and suddenly I know intuitively what the thing is about to do.

I drop and roll and spring up as, in a slithery scissoring of long and knuckled limbs, the creature crosses the distance that I have put between us and lands in the precise spot that I vacated, quicker than a cat.

As it turns to face me, I see that something extraordinary has happened to its forehead. Protruding from the center of its brow is what appears to be a tapered horn about four inches long, half an inch wide at the base but as pointed as a nail. No, not a horn, but a hollow probe of some kind from which depends a single drop of fluid as red as blood. The droplet falls, and the segmented horn collapses into itself, backward into the skull. At the point where it retracted is a small puckered pouch of skin that I had not previously noticed.

The creature doesn't mean to kill me. I am to be converted, as was the woman, into a servant and defender of whatever Norris Hiskott has become.

Twenty-five

AGAIN I KNOW, I MOVE, DUCK, CLAMBER ACROSS
a club chair, and the creature is where I was an instant
earlier, turning toward me with a hiss of anger and
frustration.

I continue moving, circling the pool table, keeping it
between us, as the few remaining moths take flight again
and caper about the chandelier, their distorted shadows
chasing silverfish across the green felt.

Following his hybrid rebirth, Hiskott has become argu-
ably psychic, in the sense that he can have out-of-body
experiences and invade the minds of others; therefore, this
beast that serves him may have some such ability to a
lesser degree. In fact, the compulsion that I feel to stare
into those milky eyes suggests that an attempt is being

made to cast a sort of spell and render me incapable of flight or self-defense.

Because of my gifts, this creature has no more power over me than does Norris Hiskott. But maybe its attempt to fix me in place with a psychic skewer, like a lepidopterist pinning a butterfly to a specimen board, opens a channel between us that transmits the beast's intentions to me.

Then I realize that I've missed more than one opportunity to kill the thing. Worse, I no longer have the pistol in a two-hand grip. I've allowed the muzzle to drift off target. To a degree, I'm susceptible to the creature's unspoken suggestions, after all.

Bringing the gun up, both hands on the grip, I fail to move when my adversary does, and abruptly it looms over me, seizing my head in both bony hands, to hold me steady for the sting. It stinks of burnt matches, rotting roses. The milky eyes are two chalices of steaming anesthetic and bitter venom. A strong supple scaly tail, previously unnoticed, whips around my legs. The capelike mass of loose skin billows out and then forward to enwrap my body, as if I am soon to be a monk of its satanic order, robed and cowled and moon-eyed alike to it.

The first shot takes the beast point-blank in the chest.

Its grip on my skull only tightens. The dripping hornlike probe extrudes from its brow. It rears back its Gorgon head, the better to slam the horn through my skull, linking brain to brain.

Trapped between us, angled upward, the gun discharges, gouging a gout of flesh and splintered wedge of jawbone from the fiend's face, instantly collapsing its grin of triumph.

The hideous cape of skin slips away from me, the tail unwinds from my legs, one calloused clammy hand slides along my face, but yet the creature's head darts down to gore my brow.

Fired into that red-toothed and howling mouth, the third bullet spares me by coring the brain, shattering through the back of the head, and drilling into the ceiling. The curiously articulated legs fold this way and that, the hooked hands seem to seek a grip upon the air, and the beast drops, falls back, faceup, no luster any longer in its eyes, the cape of skin, like a mortuary shroud, draping its body.

It lies still except for the rolled collar of excess skin around its neck. Perhaps in some postmortem reflex, that dark-gray rouleau unspools, insinuates itself between the carpet and the broken skull, and creeps across the top of the head, over the brow, and down the face, whereupon it quivers and becomes as lifeless as the visage that it covers, as though the creature had been given license to walk the Earth on the condition that in both life and death it recognize the shame of its appearance and its purpose.

From the cellar rises an inhuman cry that might be an expression of rage, although to me it is more like a lamentation, a sorrowing, woven through with bright threads of sharp anxiety. This is a cry of madness, as well, of melancholy alienation from all that might give comfort.

I could pity what mourns and cowers in the darkness below, if I didn't expect that it was another like the one I just killed and that, given the chance, it would induct me into their hive.

As the plaintive cries subside, I consider sitting and waiting for Hiskott and the third of his guards to come looking for me rather than risk searching further, when behind every closed door might wait a thief of minds and a collector of souls. But the insect-infested furniture isn't appealing, and the deeply unwholesome atmosphere will corrode courage if I linger too long.

The stench of burnt matches and rotten roses clings to me, and I feel soiled by the touch of those hands and the embrace of that cape. I would like nothing more than to wash my hands and face, but even if I dare to delay to scrub away the smell, I don't trust even the water in this place to be safe and pure.

In the foyer once more, I stand listening to the house. A pool of silence, fathoms deep, it is not stirred by any current, with not a ripple to disturb its surface.

As I climb the stairs, the treads softly complain, marking

my position step by step. But retreat is no more an option than was standing still.

Four rounds left in the pistol. Six in the revolver, which rides uncomfortably in the small of my back, cylinder pressing hard against my spine.

Even now, as I ascend from the first floor to the second, I feel as if I am descending, as if there is no up in this house, no forward or back, no sideways, only *down*. The strict laws of nature have not been suspended here. The strong perception of ascent as descent is either an illusion, a psychological reaction to the singular threat I face, or something similar to that condition called synesthesia, when a certain sound will be perceived as a color and a certain odor as a sound. Or maybe this phenomenon is related to Hiskott and what he has become, an effect of some aura that surrounds him. The feeling is so unsettling that I need one hand for the railing.

I reach the landing. Nothing waits on the second flight or, as far as I can see, at the head of the stairs.

Ascending, I am no longer able to look at the treads before me, because they actually *appear* to lead back to the first floor, even though I can tell from the flex and strain of calves and thighs that I am climbing.

Off the stairs, forward along the corridor, the floor seems to have a steep downward slope, although I know that it does not. The ceiling appears to lower, the walls tilt at queer angles, and the architecture, at least as I perceive it, becomes that of a carnival funhouse.

The purpose of this illusion, projected upon me by my psychic quarry, is not merely to confuse me and make me more vulnerable, but also to funnel me directly toward the room in which he waits. Ahead, the ceiling bends to meet the floor and block further progress, the wall to my left shifts toward me, pressing me sharply to the right, to a threshold. Beyond an open door, the ruler of Harmony Corner lies abed in a four-poster, attended by his third servant.

The creature standing is much like the one that I encountered in the library, though what human features remain of the original motor-court guest are those of a man. The mottled-gray cloak of loose skin writhes around it as if stirred by a strong draft, though I suspect that billowing expresses its anger and anxiety.

My anxiety is no less acute. My heart beats like a stallion's hooves, my breast filled with the sound of iron shoes pounding hard-packed earth. Pouring sweat renews the stench of burnt matches and rotten roses in the alien oils on my skin and in my hair.

Hiskott, hybrid of man and monster, lies in glistening greasy knots of self-affection, in sloppy spills of slowly writhing coils that crush the mattress, a great pale snake with a man's features in an oversized head that is elongated like a serpent's skull. Of his six arms and six hands, four are clearly coextensive with the sinuous convolutions of the life form from another world that he once dissected and with the stem cells of which he hoped to much improve himself. The middle pair of arms are human, but those two hands are ceaselessly grasping, while the alien hands move languidly, stroking the air as if conducting an unseen orchestra through a song in a slow tempo.

My perception of devolution and degeneracy, which overcame me in the kitchen following the discovery of the rat skeletons, is confirmed here. This thing in the bed is neither a creature capable of traveling between stars nor the brilliant scientist who was a key figure in Project Polaris. This is genetic chaos, perhaps the worst of both species: Hiskott's troubled mind intact but further twisted by alien perspectives, cold alien desires, and alien powers; the body largely one best suited to another planet, perhaps grown freakishly immense and grotesque because the needs and hungers of two species have rendered it insatiable.

The bedroom reeks worse than the cellar in which I locked the other servant thing. Piled in far corners are cascades of bones from all manner of animals, and the floor around the bed is littered with fresh and spoiled meat, upon both of which this Hiskott seems content to dine. The butchered beef and pork and veal, the prepared chickens and plastic trays of fish fillets were obviously provided through the family's restaurant, although nothing seems to have been cooked, as what is still not consumed is raw.

Among this disgusting buffet are also the carcasses of animals, some partly eaten: a coyote stiff and sneering, rabbits as limp as rag piles, ground squirrels, rats. Perhaps in the night, especially when the moon is waning and no one at the distant motor court is likely to glimpse a fleet nightmarish figure in the rolling meadows, the thing I killed in the library or this one here, or the one in the cellar, goes hunting for its master. I wonder that there haven't been more feasts of human flesh than only Maxy—but perhaps there have been. No one could know what hobo or coastal hiker, or what itinerant homeless person camping for the night on the beach, might have been overcome, paralyzed with venom or by a brain spiking, and dragged secretly to this chamber not to serve but to *be* served.

Upon catching sight of me, as I stand trembling on the threshold of this abattoir, Hiskott lifts his huge head, which must be at least three times the size of any man's head, yet is recognizably human. He opens his wide greedy mouth of ragged teeth in what appears to be a silent scream but is instead a call. The call is psychic, a command—*Feed me*—and I feel it pulling at me as a riptide pulls a swimmer under, into drowning depths.

Hiskott's confidence is palpable, the kind of self-assurance that is a vicious courage, arrogance born of absolute power and of endless abuses never punished. I discover that I have moved off the threshold, into the room. After two or three steps, I halt as a great rustling noise arises and quickly swells louder behind me, and I am suddenly afraid that the servant in the cellar has gotten free and rises now at my back, to fold me in its cape.

Twenty-six

BEFORE I CAN LOOK OVER MY SHOULDER TO glimpse my fate, the source of the loud rustling noise becomes manifest as hundreds of moths swarm into the bedroom from the hallway, seething past me, buffeting the back of my neck, my face, questing at the corners of my mouth, at my nostrils, dusting my eyelashes with their powdery substance, fluttering through my hair and away, a surging river of soft wings.

In this house, one horror breeds another, and the swarm flies straight into Hiskott's silent scream, down into his long throat, so tender that he has no need to shred them with his teeth. Still they come, hundreds more—the house is a moth farm, their grazing among the mildewed books perhaps encouraged—and I hunch my neck to prevent them from crawling under my collar. They feed the beast on the bed, and although their numbers would seem great enough to choke it, a peristaltic pulsing in the sinuous coils suggests that the insects are easily accommodated, crushed and pushed along into the winding catacombs of the serpent's stomach.

This vile spectacle so stuns me that, as the last of the swarm answers the call, I break free of Hiskott's psychic grip, and raise the pistol. The servant thing springs toward me, horn extruding from its brow. I cut it down with the last four rounds in the magazine and throw the gun aside.

Hiskott seems unfazed that I have dispatched two of his three defenders. Having swallowed all that came to him, he preens the moth powder from his lips, from his six hands, watching me as he licks and licks. Were his tongue forked and thin, like that of a snake, it would be much less repulsive than the large, long, but human tongue that instead journeys through his many supple fingers and cleans his upturned palms.

The six arms remind me of deities like the Indian goddess Kali. Although he is wingless, there is something about him that suggests a dragon as much as a serpent. The ragged mouth of wicked teeth might give Beowulf pause. The myths and legends of many ages and kingdoms seem here combined in a single threat, a thing as self-satisfied and vain as the first of all evils that lies curled in the pit of the world.

When I draw the revolver from the small of my back, he stops licking his hands, but he does not seem alarmed. His lack of fear is unnerving, and I wish at least that he would, in all his coils, recoil. He is such a grotesque mass of thick undulations of pale scaly flesh, such a slowly writhing tanglement of involutions and convolutions, spiraled and helixed, kinked and twisted, that he appears incapable of any but the most ponderous movement, surely not a fraction as quick as any ordinary snake. Therefore, his calm seems to indicate either that he is too comfortable in his long-uncontested power or that he is more lithe than I assume.

When I raise the weapon, he proves not quick but cunning. Each time that he has invaded my mind, I have at once thrown him out. For a while, the psychic call with which he attracted the moths was also effective with me, but I somehow know—as he seems to know as well—that it will not work again.

As I take two steps closer to the bed and line up the first of what I hope will be six head shots, steadying my hands and my aim with considerable effort, Hiskott throws his last trick at me, and it is his best yet. I don't know how he learned my real name, how he discovered what wound of mine has never healed and never will. Maybe he has a way to go online, to search for the truth of me as did Jolie's new friend Ed. He does not try to crawl into my head as before but with tremendous mental power casts into my mind the most beautiful face I've ever known, Stormy Llewellyn as she lived and breathed.

I am rocked backward a step by such a vivid image of my girl flaring through my mind's eye. It seems a desecration of her memory even to think about her in this disgusting hole, but round two of his assault is worse. He imagines her as she might have looked a few days after death, with the lividity and bloat of a corpse, and he throws that picture at me, which almost drops me to my knees.

If he could move quickly, I might be dead even as my knees go weak at the sight of Stormy's face corrupted. But he is sliding off the bed with sluglike sloth, and he makes the mistake of blasting more images at me of Stormy in advanced stages of decomposition, so grievous and dispiriting that they jolt me to the realization that Stormy was cremated within a day of death. She was pure, and she was purified by fire, and nothing that feeds on the dead ever fed on her or ever will.

Six hollow-point copper-jacketed cartridges from a .38 revolver can take apart a dragon's head with finality, especially when each is fired from closer range than the one before it, the last with the muzzle pressed against the hateful skull.

That would have been the end of it, if I had but remembered that due to the fact that its nerves will fire for a while after death, a beheaded snake can still thrash as vigorously as one that is alive.

Twenty-seven

AS ANYONE KNOWS WHO HAS SEEN A HEADLESS snake lash away the ghost of life that still inhabits its mortal coils, the decapitated body seems to whip more dramatically than it ever could have done when it was part of a complete creature. The same is true of the Hiskott-alien hybrid. In bed, he was a flaccid mass of obscene love knots, writhing as lazily as worms in cold earth; but with his brains blown out, he is the crazed colossal squid from *Twenty Thousand Leagues Under the Sea*, and he seems to be not one great length of scaly muscle but instead a nest of powerful tentacles whipping in a destructive frenzy.

The transformation occurs with the sixth and final gunshot, when his impossibly tangled body untangles with an eruption of energy that might have been stored in it for the past five years. I am swept off my feet, though not in a romantic sense, and thrown all the way back to the door by which I entered. I crash just short of the threshold, rapping my head on the hardwood floor, a blow that no doubt does more damage to the floor than to my skull, though for a moment my vision swims.

I'm seeing double for a couple of seconds, but when my vision clears, it seems that the big room is filled almost wall to wall with a furious snake seeking pieces of its shattered head to puzzle back together and live again. Great muscled coils snap the thick posts of the canopy bed as though they are made of balsa wood. Lamps fly and shatter, red brocade draperies are torn from windows to flare and fan as if the decapitated serpent is both bullfighter and bull, and those cascades of bones that slope to the ceiling in some corners are slung in every direction in rattling barrages of skeletal fragments.

Before I might be knocked unconscious by a ham bone, which seems so apt as to be inevitable, I scramble across the threshold, into the upstairs hall, and thrust to my feet.

To be certain beyond a doubt that this extraterrestrial anaconda will eventually spasm into a final stillness, as would any snake of this world, I need to bear witness. But I can do that safely from the midfloor landing of the stairs and return for visual confirmation after this furious thrashing ceases.

As I turn toward the stairs, I am more than dismayed to see the third of Hiskott's caped and horned servants ascending after having escaped the cellar. It is as quick and agile as the beast in the library, springing toward me with murderous intent, and I am without a handgun.

Just then, the headless stump of the Hiskott hybrid surges out of the bedroom, its six arms grasping blindly, like something that Francisco Goya, Hieronymus Bosch, Henry Fuseli, and Salvador Dalí might have painted in collaboration after eating too many oysters followed by a night of heavy drinking. The questing hands seize the servant thing. The serpent uncoils into the hallway and coils again around the creature it has snared, crushing the life out of it as the greedy hands tear off its head.

I retreat to the farther end of the hallway to watch the death throes of Harmony Corner's tyrannical ruler. After a minute or so, the dramatic flailing subsides, the great thick length of the serpent ravels down upon itself in pale folds, like a deflated fire hose, and lies shuddering, twitching, until no trace current remains in its neural pathways.

When the creature has been completely still for five minutes, I am brave enough to approach it, although not foolish enough to make a disparaging remark about my vanquished enemy. Modern movies don't contain a lot of truth. But this one lesson I've learned from them has proved to be as true as anything in my curious life: When you stand over the dead monster and, full of bravado, make a wisecrack, the monster will rise up, not dead after all, and make a last furious assault. In half of those movies, it kills one of the few remaining survivors. As I am the only survivor present, I figure that a single wisecrack cuts in half my chances of getting out of this house alive. If I am the equivalent of Tom Cruise, I will surely exit unscathed. If I am the equivalent of Harry Dean Stanton or Paul Reiser or Wayne Knight, which I figure is far closer to the truth, then I'm well advised to keep my mouth shut and tread lightly.

I try to find places to step between the coils, but sometimes I have to step on them and clamber across them. I hold my tongue, keep my balance, and leave behind pale mounds of snake flesh that would be a feast for a roc, the giant bird of Arabian myth that eats snakes—among other things. The way events have been unfolding in the Corner, there's every reason to suppose a roc—or a flock of them—might be in the neighborhood.

As I'm pretty sure that the Jeep Grand Cherokee is not in any condition to be driven out of the house, I leave by the front door. In the distance, the smoke is lifting. Through the haze, I can see the fire trucks, streams of water arcing.

In the front yard stand Jolie's parents, Bill and Ardys Harmony, and three other people whom I don't know but who must be, I assume, members of the family. From their hopeful yet wary expressions, I can only conclude that they have felt Hiskott disconnect his open line to their minds.

As I reach the head of the steps, something in a pocket of my jeans squirms vigorously, and I cry out in alarm, because baby snakes can be as venomous as adults. Those on the lawn cry out, as well, and take a step backward. Fishing the thing from my pocket, I smile sheepishly and say, "Just the cell phone."

I take the call. It's Ed.

Twenty-eight

SOME OF THE FIELDS ARE BLACK WITH VEINS of gray ashes, but no buildings have been lost to the fire I set. When the wind blows away the last lingering wisps of smoke, the odor of burnt things is less sour than I expect, rather like a campfire smell.

Sawhorses are placed at the entrance to the Corner, bearing hand-lettered signs that declare CLOSED 24 HOURS FOR FIRE CLEANUP.

Tomorrow, heavy equipment will come to remove the eighteen-wheeler from the meadow.

The family's tow truck has been brought down from the service station, and the Grand Cherokee has been hauled to the grove of oaks in which the three vehicles that once belonged to Hiskott's servants are hidden.

Among them, the Harmony family has six of those three-gallon emergency-supply containers of gasoline. Once filled at the station, they are lined up on the porch of the residence that Hiskott took for his own.

In the afternoon, after the breeze dies out, after we shut down the electric supply at the breaker box and cut off the propane feed, Bill Harmony and I enter the house. Starting on the top floor, we pour gasoline in strategic places, especially over the remains of the hybrids. I keep Bill out of the kitchen, so that he will not see the small skeleton in the pantry.

The lights don't work in the reeking cellar, and I choose not to descend into that gloom with a flashlight. I empty the sixth can down the steps, into that sinister darkness. The gasoline fumes are overwhelming. The house is a bomb waiting for the fuse to be lit.

The family has used its half-size tanker truck, the white rig with HARMONY CORNER in big red letters, to hose down the six houses below the one that we will burn. Refilled, it stands ready nearby to keep this new fire from spreading to the unburned fields.

We set the house alight an hour before sunset. At night, the conflagration would be more visible from the Coast Highway, and some traveler would be more likely to report it to authorities.

Annamaria and I gather with the family to watch.

Thirty-six of them are present, including Jolie, who has returned from Fort Wyvern. The flames are satisfying, and I use Purvis Beamer's smartphone to send a video of the blaze to Ed.

No one cheers the fire. Indeed, they watch mostly in silence, and if the atmosphere of the event is like anything else, it is most like an hour in church.

When the house is smouldering ruins and the embers have been watered down, we all gather on the beach, where picnic tables and folding chairs have been set up for dinner. The air is cool enough for sweaters and jackets, but everyone agrees that the beach is the best place for this first meal of their new freedom.

The waxing moon and many candles provide enough light, because this is only the dark of nature and not to be feared. The waves are low, breaking gently along the coast as if shushing crying children to sleep.

The stars are a grand display that lifts my heart. Considering Project Polaris, I expect those far suns and their distant worlds to seem a little threatening this night, but instead they say to me that the vast universe, like Earth itself, is a place of promise that is no less magnificent for the fact that it is also a field of contest upon which the one struggle was fought, is fought, and will be fought from the beginning of time until time is ended.

Dinner on the beach is less solemn than the vigil at the

burning house, but remains a quiet celebration. Many smiles and just a little laughter. This extended family has been through great suffering and humiliation, and the way back to a normal life will not be an easy road.

These are good people, and I make new friends here. They hug a lot, and when they take my hand or lay a hand upon my shoulder, they often are reluctant to let go. But they understand intuitively that they must not embarrass me with gratitude. Although they obviously realize that I have many secrets to keep, they don't press to know them, but seem satisfied that I should be always a mystery, as are so many things in this life.

After dinner, Jolie and Annamaria and I and the two dogs—Raphael and Boo—walk together along the beach, near the foaming surf, and the girl is quietly enraptured with everything she sees, everything she hears, everything she thinks. Now that the yoke of slavery is lifted from her and from her family, I am able to see more clearly the brilliance, the courage, and the pure heart that form the essence of her. I can imagine the woman she will become, and the world could use uncounted millions like her, though just one will make a difference.

Jolie comes to tears at the thought that we will be leaving in the morning and that we may never see one another again. That such a bond can form in but a day bewilders her, as it delights me, and she is afraid that her life, now recaptured, will prove to be marked more by parting and loss than she can bear. I am, she says, like her new brother, and brothers can't go away forever. She is a girl who feels things strongly, and though cynics might mock her for that, I never will, as it is perhaps the best of graces: to feel deeply, to care profoundly.

In my bones, I know that I am not long for this world. The life I have led and must lead brings Death and me face-to-face with such regularity that I, as imperfect a man as any other, will sooner or later fail whatever higher power it is that has sent me on this series of missions. Therefore, I can't lie to Jolie and say we will see each other again in this world.

Annamaria soothes away the girl's tears as I cannot. She says that each of us has his or her role in life, and if we know ourselves well enough to understand what that role is, we will be happy doing nothing else but what we can do best. She says that I, Odd Thomas, fully understand my role—a statement with which I might argue on some other occasion. She tells Jolie that I am one of those wanderers of legend, who goes where he feels he must and, in the going, finds those who need him, and in finding those who need him, fulfills his destiny. This sounds more grand to me than the truth of my life, but this touch of myth enchants the girl and mellows her sadness with mystery.

Somehow, Annamaria knows that Jolie's mother, in homeschooling, assigns her many writing assignments of all kinds. She suggests that the girl write down her part of the story in which we have recently been involved and that she mail it to me, care of Ozzie Boone, my writer friend in Pico Mundo, so that when I compose my account of the events in Harmony Corner, I can include Jolie's point of view. When she hears that I have written a series of memoirs that will not be published in my lifetime, if ever, Jolie is electrified. Although she may never hold a real book of this story in her hand, only someday a copy of my manuscript, she is enchanted by the prospect—and the fact that we will continue to have a connection puts an end to her tears.

As we walk back the way we came, to rejoin the family, Annamaria says, "One thing you must remember when you're writing, Jolie. If the story you and Odd collaborate on is to be seamless, you should write just as you are, just as you talk, just as you think, and not try for some writerly voice that isn't yours. What you don't see that I do is that you and Oddie are in many ways two of a kind. You and he so love the world, in spite of all your suffering, that you are in what some might call a heightened state of consciousness. You and Oddie embrace so much with such great enthusiasm, that one thing reminds you of a dozen others, your mind is here and there and also *there* at the same time, but you are never scatterbrained, you are focused nonetheless. Look up the word *discursive*. When you write, keep that word in mind, and then your words and Oddie's will flow together. Be of the world and in the world and above the world all at once. Be you and only you, which means be you and all the people you have loved, and then Oddie will always be with you as, I know, you will always be with him."

Annamaria doesn't seem concerned about drying *my* tears.

In spite of the chill, no one wants to bring the gathering to an end, but it comes to an end just the same.

Back in Cottage 7, I take a long hot shower even though I showered earlier, between leaving Hiskott's house and returning to burn it down.

Raphael stays the night with me, and Boo goes wherever it is he has to go. A good dog is a comfort. The golden retriever comforts me, and perhaps Boo comforts someone in a place that I can't imagine. I leave a lamp on, but I do not dream.

When I wake near dawn, I lie listening to Raphael snore, and I find myself considering what it means to be fallen. We are fallen in a broken world, and one thing that occurs to me is that after thousands of years, when we think of fallen angels, we think of them as we always have: busy spreading misery on Earth. But the universe in its immensity is nevertheless of a piece, and what applies at one end of it applies at the other. No doubt misery, like happiness and hope, is found throughout the stars. The alien artifacts housed in Fort Wyvern are of extraterrestrial origin, but perhaps they are at the same time part of the ancient history of humanity.

I shower again on rising, and afterward take a call from Ed. We agreed earlier that he will stay in touch with Jolie and be her secret friend, but that he will not again allow her through that last pair of steel doors, into Wyvern. We say our good-byes. His last words to me are "Live long and prosper." Mine to him are "Open the pod bay doors, HAL," and I think he laughs.

Leaving, Annamaria drives the Mercedes we have borrowed from Hutch Hutchison in Magic Beach. Along the last length of blacktop leading to the county road, thirty-six members of the Harmony family stand side by side, waiting for us, which I wish they would not have done. Jolie stands with her mother and father and her uncle Donny at the end of the line. She waves. I wave.

The Coast Highway takes us south toward what will prove to be a place called Roseland, which will be far worse than Harmony Corner in its worst days. In Roseland, I will have to put Jolie entirely out of my mind, for to think of her, in all her vulnerability, out there in this world of corruption, would perhaps paralyze me. And I have work to do.